I0718059

His Majesty's Hounds – Book 6

Sweet and Clean Regency Romance

Redeeming the Marquess

Arietta Richmond

Dreamstone Publishing © 2017

www.dreamstonepublishing.com

ISBN: 1925499677

ISBN-13: 978-1-925499-67-4

Disclaimer

This story is a work of fiction.

Names, characters, places and incidents are the product of the author's imagination and are used fictitiously. Any resemblance to events, locales or actual persons, living or dead, is entirely coincidental.

Some actual historical events of the period may be referenced in passing.

Books by Arietta Richmond

His Majesty's Hounds

Claiming the Heart of a Duke

Intriguing the Viscount

Giving a Heart of Lace
(a prequel to Winning the Merchant Earl)

Being Lady Harriet's Hero

Enchanting the Duke

Redeeming the Marquess

Finding the Duke's Heir

Winning the Merchant Earl (coming soon)

Healing Lord Barton (coming soon)

Loving the Bitter Baron (coming soon)

Rescuing the Countess (coming soon)

Attracting the Spymaster (coming soon)

Other Books

The Scottish Governess (coming soon)

The Earl's Reluctant Fiancée (coming soon)

The Crew of the Seadragon's Soul Series,
(coming soon - a set of 10 linked novels)

The Derbyshire Set

A Gift of Love (Prequel short story)

A Devil's Bargain (Prequel short story - coming soon)

The Earl's Unexpected Bride

The Captain's Compromised Heiress

The Viscount's Unsuitable Affair

The Derbyshire Set, Omnibus Edition, Volume 1
(contains the first three books in a single volume.)

The Count's Impetuous Seduction

The Rake's Unlikely Redemption

The Marquess' Scandalous Mistress

The Derbyshire Set, Omnibus Edition, Volume 2
(contains the second three books in a single volume.)

A Remembered Face (Bonus short story – coming soon)

The Marchioness' Second Chance (coming soon)

A Viscount's Reluctant Passion (coming soon)

Lady Theodora's Christmas Wish

The Duke's Improper Love (coming soon)

Dedication

For everyone who had the grace to be patient while this book, and every other book that I have written, was coming into existence, who provided cups of tea, and food, when the writing would not let me go, and endured countless times being asked for opinions.

For the readers who inspire me to continue writing, by buying my books! Especially for those of you who have taken the time to email me, or to leave reviews, and tell me what you love about these books, and what you'd like to see more of – thank you – I'm listening, I promise to write more about your favourite characters.

For my growing team of beta readers and advance reviewers – it's thanks to you that others can enjoy these books in the best presentation possible!

And for all the writers of Regency Historical Romance, whose books I read, who inspired me to write in this fascinating period.

Table of Contents

Chapter One

The Berkshire countryside, England, April 1816

Philip Canterwood, Duke of Rotherhithe, surveyed his drawing room with some displeasure.

It was full of a mixed collection of young men, all happy to consume his food, and his excellent wines. He sighed. This was, like it or not, the best to be found as far as eligible young men of noble blood. The ending of the war may have eased things somewhat, but the impact of 20 years of fighting was clearly to be seen. Why was it that it seemed always the best men were the ones to die, and the fools the ones who survived?

He had to hope that at least one of these men was going to suit young Georgiana. They were all of impeccable breeding, titled and supposedly wealthy (although one could never be entirely sure). It was only the quality of their behaviour that gave him concern.

He had promised his bride-to-be's father, on his deathbed, that he would see his younger daughter successfully wed to a man of quality. He intended to fulfil that promise. Unfortunately, she was intelligent, and stubborn – he suspected that, to actually get her to wed, unless a miracle happened, he might have to force her hand. It was not an idea he liked.

Still, a month of these rapacious young men eating his food, and drinking his wine, should give them a suitable chance to impress her – surely, surely, one would take her fancy?

Ah well, he would see soon enough. Cordelia and Georgiana would arrive this evening. He could barely wait to see Cordelia again. He still could not quite believe how lucky he was, to have found love a second time in his life, and with such a beautiful young woman.

He left the young men to their wine and conversation, and went to ensure that all arrangements were in place for his Lady's arrival.

~~~~~

Oliver Kentworthy, Marquess of Dartworth, was equally unhappy with the company he found himself in, in the Duke of Rotherhithe's drawing room. Had the opportunity for discussion arisen, the two men would have been surprised to find themselves so much in agreement.

Oliver found the young noblemen who surrounded him to be remarkably shallow and opinionated, without any substance to support those opinions. He felt, unsurprisingly after his last few years, utterly out of place.
~~~~~

He had been surprised to be invited, and was not at all sure that attending had been a wise choice. Time would tell. Given that they were all ignoring him, he suspected that the weeks ahead would not be enjoyable.

At the earliest opportunity, he removed himself to the peace of the library.

~~~~~

The mud was thick and wet and stuck to the carriage wheels like sticky, dark molasses.

"If this road becomes any rougher, I am entirely convinced that we shall break a wheel and be stuck in the mud for days and days to come."

Lady Cordelia Branley sighed deeply and looked more than a little seasick as she perched unsteadily inside the rolling carriage and wondered how her beautiful younger sister could so easily endure the constant jostling and jarring discomfort.

Even more so, she envied Miss Millpost, their long-term companion, her ability to actually sleep under such conditions.

"It can't be much further, Cordelia. An hour at most and we should be at Canterwood Park. I'm sure the road will improve as we get closer." Georgiana drew a strand of fine blond hair from across her face and smiled at her sister, hoping to cheer her up when she felt no joy herself at leaving her beloved family home.

"I know it's been terribly hard since Papa passed away, dear Cordelia."
~~~~~

The carriage lurched in and out of a deep rut and the two Ladies nearly fell off their seats. After taking a moment to regain her balance, Georgiana continued speaking.

"And now we have to leave our lovely house so that you can marry the Duke and I can find a husband."

She frowned and pursed her full lips.

"But why on earth did Papa arrange things in such a way? I would never have left the estate if Papa had not placed that annoying clause in his will. It is entirely vexatious to have to marry before I may come into my inheritance fully!"

"Oh, Georgiana. Don't speak of Papa in such a way. He was only thinking of our happiness. He knew it would be difficult for us to manage on our own and only wanted to be sure that we both found good husbands."

The evening was drawing in and a shadow fell across the delicate curve of Georgiana's fine cheekbones. Cordelia gasped as the carriage lurched once again. She was feeling tired and was worried about her appearance after the arduous coach journey. She wanted to look her best for her future husband.

"I, for one, am grateful for my good fortune. I have not only found love, but I am to be the Duchess of Rotherhithe. You know that the Duke is a very kind and wealthy man. He will take very good care of your inheritance until such time as you are married."

Georgiana pulled the carriage blanket about her and shook her head.

"I know I could have taken care of everything myself. With or without a husband!"

Cordelia was slightly shocked at her sister's unladylike sense of independence.

Whilst she had to admit that Georgiana had shown remarkable dedication to learning everything that she could about estate management in the months since their father's death, she still could not quite comprehend why Georgiana would *want* to do everything herself.

"Papa only wanted the best for you, Georgie, and you know that you can return to the house whenever you want, once you have a new husband - just as soon as you've spoken your wedding vows."

"But your dear Duke has already appointed a farm manager to help the estate manager run Casterfield Grange in our absence and he's even sent over another gardener to look after the grounds. I only hope that they know enough between them to make sure that my flower beds are properly tended. I've worked so hard to cultivate the rose bushes and now a pair of complete strangers are trampling all over my precious flowers in their muddy boots. It just isn't fair!"

"Philip is more than a Duke, Georgiana. Unlike many titled men, he actually cares about his lands and people, just like Papa did. He understands these things. He knows how to run an estate. He's been doing it for years."

"Well, he's certainly had enough years of practice." There was a slightly hard, sulky edge to Georgiana's voice.

Philip Canterwood, the Duke of Rotherhithe, was nearly twenty-five summers older than Cordelia, and Georgiana, in her tiredness, was not so subtly referring to that fact.

A silence fell between the two sisters as the cool, damp air pinched at their cheeks and made them pull their carriage blankets closer to their chins.

"Oh Delia, I do worry about you sometimes. I know that you say you love the Duke, and I'm sure you do, but really, are you quite sure about marrying a man so much older than you?"

"Of course, silly. I do love him, very much, and he loves me. And he's such a sweet and kind gentleman - I just know in my heart that I'm going to be happy with him."

"But he's already an old man, dearest sister. Doesn't that concern you in any way?"

Cordelia laughed. "He's not so old you know. Forty-two isn't really old. He's in the prime of life – he's strong and handsome, and well respected. Why would that worry me? And... younger men are somehow better? Is that what you're implying?"

Georgiana had no practical experience on the subject of the quality of men, so she simply looked down at the carriage floor. The carriage bounced and shuddered along the rutted, muddy highway. Miss Millpost snored gently, propped against the corner of the seat.

"Papa said it was always better to be an old man's sweetheart than a young man's plaything!"

Georgiana looked thoughtful at that, then shrugged. "I don't think I want to be anyone's sweetheart or plaything. I just want to go home. How long am I really expected to stay at the Duke's, Cordelia? It's such a terrible nuisance to be wrenched away from home like this. Surely, once your wedding is done, I can go home, even if I haven't found anyone to marry by then?"

"I'm sure you'll find someone to marry. Papa left the house and the farmlands to you, Georgiana. He was a Baron and you're a Baron's daughter. You're quite the catch, you know – there will be gentlemen falling at your feet, given that you have a rich dowry, and you're pretty. The house and the lands will be yours as soon as you're wedded, and, even though they will stay yours, as Papa willed it, your new husband will get the benefit of the good income the property will produce. It really couldn't be simpler. Your fate, my darling sister, is in your own hands – you just have to get on with choosing a man and marrying him. And Philip will make sure that you make a good match."

Cordelia smiled, with all the warmth her heart could muster in the cramped conditions of the draughty coach.

The unspoken truth was that so many young men of noble blood had taken service in His Majesty's forces to fight the French, and never come home, that there was, to some extent, rather a shortage of eligible young men.

The wars had dragged on for nearly twenty years and the Army and Navy had swallowed up a generation of young men, despatching them to fight in so many wars in faraway places. Whilst the war was now ended, over its course it had taken many, many lives - by disease, musket fire, cannon volleys and the cuts and slashes of sabre blades.

Many young women despaired of ever finding a husband at all, especially a man with all his limbs and eyes intact, who was still on the right side of sixty.

Yes, there were still eligible bachelors to be found, but the competition for strong-limbed, blue-blooded and landed young men was fierce indeed.

Too many of the young men from the great houses, who had managed to return from war unscathed, or escaped its touch altogether, were more inclined to squander their fortunes at the gaming tables, drinking and carousing, all too aware of how short and cruel life could be. They preferred to play rather than apply themselves to the arduous business of running their estates.

Georgiana felt instinctively repelled by such callow behaviour. She would much prefer to remain on her own than be saddled with some crowing fool who only sought the pleasures of brandy and cards in the smoke-filled salons of disreputable hostesses. It really was a fate too terrible to contemplate. The thought sometimes made her weep with frustration. There had to be a better way – it was so unfair that women were expected to be ruled in all things by men.

In the growing darkness of the carriage's cramped interior, Georgiana's thoughts strayed to the days of her childhood, when life had been far simpler and easier to deal with. She wished things were simple now. She wished she were back at Casterfield Grange, the house she loved and the lands she'd grown up on, the rich agricultural farm lands she'd learned to care for, and manage. All her memories where there – she barely remembered living anywhere else. The girls had lost their mother when they were small children; Georgiana had been only five and her sister barely seven at the time.

Although there had been beautiful portraits of their mother on the walls of Tillingford Castle, which now graced the halls of Casterfield Grange, neither of the girls could really remember her.

The society beauty who had become the dazzling Baroness Tillingford was a faint memory of warm arms and the scent of roses, but little more. They'd had nurses, governesses, maids and companions. But no mother.

Yet both girls had been most fortunate to inherit their mother's fine looks. The early loss of their mother had drawn the two sisters into a close and unbreakable bond of kinship. Cordelia, the taller of the two, had always been deeply fond of her little sister. She'd always felt very protective towards her. She also wondered, sometimes, if the absence of a mother had made Georgiana a little too headstrong and stubborn for a Lady of her rank and position.

But Georgiana was an intelligent young woman with a quick mind and an extremely capable brain. Her father had happily indulged her interest in books by hiring Miss Millpost, a strict but perceptive woman, as governess, and then a tutor to teach her something of the classics. Miss Millpost had spotted a kindred soul in the young child and happily taught her chess, encouraging the curious and critical young mind to flourish and develop in ways that might have shocked the other members of the local aristocracy.

Miss Millpost was a stickler for propriety, but also saw no reason that a girl shouldn't use her brain. In general, girls were expected to sew and learn domestic arts like embroidery, painting watercolours, playing musical instruments, and managing the day to day activities of a household.

Often, women of rank were not even expected to be able to read, in the more traditional of families.

There were servants and maids and footmen to attend to all of the manual labours, and a Lady was expected to rule her household with firmness and disciplined good order.

She was not expected to get her delicate fingers dirty or spoil her fine gowns in the gardens. Georgiana had always been a poor fit for that image of womanhood.

She had preferred the outdoors, the stables and the gardens, collecting an impressive variety of plants and flowers. She loved to rush into her father's study with an armful of blooms, mud on her dress and feet, hands grubby from toiling in the soil and place the fragrant petals before him.

He would laugh and kiss her on her forehead and call her his pretty peasant girl, loving her light and energy and indulging her hobbies and interests. She reminded him so much of his deceased wife, who had been just such a bright and intelligent person, if not, perhaps, quite so prone to acquiring a covering of dust or mud on her clothing!

When Miss Millpost had arrived at Casterfield Grange to school Georgiana in the basics, she was also expected to coach her in the ways of gentility. In that area, she would later admit that she wasn't quite as successful as she'd originally hoped. She had imparted good advice along with the daily lessons.

"You might have to disguise your wits, young lady, for an intelligent woman is seen as both a rarity and a novelty and therefore something to be feared. But never abandon them, for they are a rare enough gift either in men or in women!"

Georgiana had studied hard and learned to appreciate her governess's warmth and encouragement, despite her strict and formal manner as they explored the Baron's extensive library.

Miss Millpost had agreed to stay with them, as companion now, rather than governess, until Georgiana was married. Shortly before the Baron died he had informed her that he had settled on her, in his will, a substantial annuity, and a cottage, in thanks for her long service. Both Cordelia and Georgiana suspected that Miss Millpost looked forward to the day of Georgiana's marriage with thorough enthusiasm, simply because it would free her to live her own life.

If she had her way, Georgiana fully intended to persuade the Duke to simply release her inheritance to her, and let her run the lands and the household on her own, rather than forcing her to marry before she could do anything. She knew that she was more than capable. She just had to persuade the Duke to see sense. She'd studied hard and understood the rules of agriculture, bookkeeping, finance and how people could flourish when relieved from poverty and oppression. Her father had always treated his tenants well, and she had seen, at first hand, how much impact that had on their lives and their productivity.

Georgiana was completely convinced that she could run her estate successfully, that she could manage the household perfectly well and make sure that the workers and tenants were properly fed and cared for. Her ideas would, most likely, never find favour with her neighbours in the surrounding estates, but she had learnt so much from Miss Millpost, from her private tutor, and from the estate manager, that she now felt a deep responsibility towards the people who lived and worked on her land. She wanted a chance to prove her worth and the only obstacle to that ambition was her sister's future husband, the Duke himself.

Whilst she had to admit that she liked the man, and that he had her best interests at heart, she was also certain that he would do his utmost to abide by her Papa's last wishes. She also had to admit that she had never really demonstrated her ability in his presence – for, until her Papa's death, she had not truly known her own heart, and had simply learned for the joy of it, with no particular purpose in mind. It was quite reasonable that he currently perceived her as a somewhat scatter-brained, if intelligent, girl.

The idea of returning to her wonderful house at Casterfield Grange as the wife of some half-wit, pretentious young nobleman from the local gentry sent shivers of dread down her spine.

At last, they approached the line of handsome poplars which marked the boundary of the Duke's estate, and Cordelia leaned out of the carriage window to catch sight of the lanterns shining atop the magnificent wrought iron gates that were being swung open to admit them. She admired the elegant gatehouse and noted the liveried servants bowing to her as the carriage passed along the gravel driveway that led to the stately house, slowing to a more comfortable pace as the coachman eased the horses to a walk.

This was her moment. She was coming to her new home. She was to be the new Duchess of Rotherhithe, with all of the lands, titles and privileges that came with marriage to Philip Canterwood, Duke of Rotherhithe.

Her share of her father's inheritance would add to the Canterwood fortune (although part would always be hers alone, as per the conditions of her father's will) and the two families would be united forever.

The only minor obstacle now, to her complete happiness, was to find a suitable match for Georgiana, her beautiful, headstrong little sister.

The wedding, due to be held just a few short weeks from now, had provided a perfect opportunity to invite every eligible bachelor of noble blood, in the Duke's very wide circle of acquaintance, to a house party, leading up to the celebration. Surely there would be enough handsome young men for one of them to catch Georgiana's fancy and, she was certain, the Duke would lend a hand in making sure that the right man was chosen. It was the least he could do to please his pretty young bride.

Her own was a match made in heaven and Cordelia was determined that her sister should have the same happiness, and be at the altar within six months of her own wedding - whatever it might take to achieve that.

Georgiana was not the only member of the Branley family with a stubborn streak!

Chapter Two

After the darkness of the countryside, it seemed that, at Canterwood Park, the lights from a thousand candles lit the many windows of the magnificent house as the carriage pulled up in front of a sweeping stone staircase, flanked by a matching pair of elegantly carved lions. The wide entrance was lit by a row of flaming torches that flared in the cool, evening breeze, casting light and shadows upon the broad, granite steps. There was a hint of late frost in the air as the horses snorted and steam curled from their sweating flanks.

Miss Millpost started awake as footmen dashed forward to open the carriage door and unfold the steps, ready to assist the Ladies as they alighted on the freshly scrubbed and swept flagstones. Cordelia almost tripped on the edge of her gown as her heel caught in a loose tangle of the decorative ribbon on her hem, but Georgiana caught her sister's arm, and the two sisters looked at each other and couldn't help laughing.

"What an entrance, dear sister," Georgiana's tone was arch, and Cordelia giggled.

Georgiana pointed at the wide, carved doors and the liveried servants scurrying to untie their luggage from the carriage's roof.

"But at least you fell in amongst good company, Cordelia!"

They laughed as they held onto each other, releasing all the tensions of the long journey, feeling quite tired after the constant pitching and rolling that had been more like a sea voyage in a tempest than a road journey by coach and four. Two sisters, still so young in so many ways, standing on the threshold of their new lives, not really knowing what the future would hold. Cordelia, poised to assume the mantle of the Duchess of Rotherhithe and Georgiana, feeling lost and uncertain of how her destiny would unfold.

Miss Millpost, standing behind them, cleared her throat pointedly.

"Perhaps, girls, we should move towards the stairs?"

There was a distinct stiffening amongst the servants and footmen as a tall and distinguished figure emerged at the top of the stairway, his polished Hessians and perfectly tailored breeches and coat of blue superfine setting off his fine figure. He smiled and revealed an even row of good teeth. His shock of thick, dark hair, given a distinguished air by the light streaking of grey at his temples, was tied back in a black silk ribbon and his eyes sparkled as he looked down at the two Ladies at the bottom of the stone steps. He raised his hands and opened his arms in a dramatic greeting.

"Venus and Aphrodite are come amongst us poor mortal men!"

Georgiana bowed her head and giggled.

"Venus and Aphrodite are the same goddess, Cordelia. Do you think his eyesight is failing?"

Cordelia, wondering inwardly why Philip was being rather more effusive than usual, nudged her sister gently in the ribs and made a graceful curtsey to acknowledge the Duke's presence above her at the top of the staircase. He stepped lightly down the stairs and waved the servants back to their tasks.

"My dear," he spoke with a warm, melodious voice. "How lovely the day has become because of your presence. Welcome to my humble abode which, by God's good grace, we shall soon be blessed to call our home together."

Georgiana stared at the older man in wonder. The Duke's 'humble abode' consisted of a hundred and fifty rooms with banqueting halls, exquisite ballrooms and some of the finest artwork and tapestries in the county. He dined off silver plate and was a confidant of the Prince Regent. Although considerably older than his bride-to-be, Philip Canterwood was still a handsome man who avoided the perils of a sedentary life by riding to hounds and hunting whenever the opportunity presented itself. He enjoyed the thrill of the chase, and his great passion was to bring down birds and small game with his highly trained falcons. Falconry might have gone somewhat out of fashion, but Philip had never let fashion dictate his actions. He had, in the past, happily whiled away many hours in the company of his treasured birds, stroking the soft feathers and plumage.

The Duke bowed courteously before Cordelia and brought her slender, gloved hand to his lips to place a gentle kiss upon the silk fabric.

The warmth of his mouth in the cold air sent a small thrill chasing along her arm and Cordelia smiled at the gesture. There was no doubt that she was thoroughly besotted with the charming Duke. It was obvious to all who had eyes to see that she was utterly certain that the distinguished gentleman before her was the love of her life. She smiled with all of her heart and the Duke seemed genuinely charmed by her grace. Clearly, Cordelia was an open book and the Duke could read her heart, mind and intentions without the slightest hint of deception. It made the young woman all the more appealing to him.

With a small inclination of his head, he turned to Georgiana and offered his greetings.

"Welcome to you too, dear Georgiana. I hope you find my home to your liking. Please feel free to enjoy its comforts for as long as you wish." He smiled at her, seeing her almost as a daughter. "But pray do not keep the young bachelors waiting too long or we'll be seeing pistols at dawn as the young bucks duel for your hand!"

She bobbed demurely in a small curtsey.

"I thank you with all my heart, your Grace, for your generous hospitality. We can but hope that enough suitors survive the culling to ask for my hand, or the county will surely run perilously short of its young nobility."

The Duke frowned for a moment as he absorbed the unexpected reply and then nodded as the girl's wit made him smile. And then he tossed back his head and laughed out loud.

"'Well, Cordelia, she has a rare wit, that pretty sister of yours. Wit and intelligence – that should be enough to catch the attention of the young men. Very good indeed!"

He was still laughing as he turned to greet Miss Millpost.

"My dear Miss Millpost – so good to see you again. It is obvious that you have been taking good care of the young Ladies!"

Miss Millpost's stern expression softened at the praise, and she curtseyed deeply.

"Why thank you, Your Grace!"

Philip took Cordelia's hand on his arm, guiding her up the broad staircase and into the welcoming light and warmth of the great house. Georgiana, with Miss Millpost at her side, followed a few paces behind, suddenly aware of how society might see her new position as the younger, unmarried sister of the future Duchess of Rotherhithe.

The grand entrance hall was lined by rows of staff in uniform, all turned out to meet their new mistress-to-be, each member of the household bowing their heads as the couple moved along the hallway and entered the library to warm themselves before a roaring fire and take a small glass of refreshment.

"A glass of madeira to warm the bones and give you an appetite for dinner, my dear?"

Cordelia smiled her assent and a servant stepped forward to pour two small glasses for the Duke and his bride-to-be.

"What about you, Georgiana, Miss Millpost? Would you care to join us in a glass?"

It seemed that the new roles were being very clearly distinguished right from the outset. The Duke and his future Duchess were served first. Everyone else had to wait their turn and would always follow at an appropriate distance behind the noble couple. Philip had not seemed so formal last year in Bath, nor when he had visited Casterfield Grange. Still she supposed it was to be expected, here, and with a houseful of guests.

Georgiana didn't really mind. As long as her sister was happy. She politely declined the Duke's invitation with a demure nod of her head. Miss Millpost, however, gratefully accepted the offer, and settled close by the fire with her glass.

Georgiana asked leave to be shown to her room so that she could unpack her baggage.

"No need for that, my girl. Your chamber maid will attend to your valise."

"Then may I be permitted to withdraw to my chamber to rest after the long journey, Your Grace? I am sure you have much to say to Cordelia without me intruding on you."

"Of course, of course, dear girl. One of the footmen will show you to your rooms. Dinner will be served at eight and I shall send someone to escort you to the dining room. We can't risk you fading away after your arduous journey, can we?"

He was obviously determined to be as genial as possible – yet there was no need – Georgiana liked the man anyway, even if she most decidedly wished that her father's last wishes had not placed her fate in his hands. She smiled politely as she turned away to be shown to her bedchamber, and to think about what she should wear for dinner on this, her first night in the Duke's magnificent house.

Her private chambers were sumptuously appointed and would have done honour to a visiting head of state. Silk brocades and rich tapestries were matched by luxurious Persian rugs.

It reminded Georgiana of a tale from The Thousand and One Nights. Never having been one to fuss much about her appearance, Georgiana decided not to waste too much effort on her decision.

She donned the first suitable gown she found, where the maid had hung it in the closet, placed a simple diamond necklace from her mother's collection around her slender neck, and wondered how she should spend the next hour or so until dinner was served.

Bored within minutes, she jumped up from her bed and resolved to explore the house and see if she could find her own way to the dining room. The concept that it might not really be appropriate for an unmarried young lady to wander the halls of a huge house, where there were a number of young men to whom she had not yet been introduced, never occurred to her.

The house was enormous by anyone's standards and Georgiana noted the vast collection of portraits that lined the walls. The Canterwood family looked down on her from their exalted, canvas positions and she hurried along past niches with polished suits of armour, and displays of ancient weapons that lined the wide, candlelit corridor.

She eventually made her way to the grand staircase which led from the upper floor to the marble reception area, an open space that was designed to welcome and impress visitors, as well as reflect the Duke's enormous wealth.

Classical statues in Italian marble were tastefully arranged around the circular entrance hall and intricate plaster mouldings graced the ceiling. Georgiana felt somewhat overwhelmed by the scale and opulence of her new surroundings. No wonder her Papa had been so keen to settle his elder daughter into such a family. This was wealth on a level that took her breath away. And all of it owned by one man. A Duke, no less. A peer of the realm. Her sister's future husband.

From the reception hall, Georgiana had the choice of three separate corridors and she stood, feeling suddenly like a small child playing a game, and pointed at each set of doors before deciding on the middle pair. As she approached, a footman bowed his head and opened the doors for her. It was still a surprise for her to see so many servants wherever she looked, as they lived very simply at Casterfield Grange, but she assumed it must be entirely normal for such a large house.

Candles had been set in glimmering silver candelabra that stood upon beautiful inlaid tables placed at intervals along the corridor. The effect was enchanting. The gentle, flickering light was reflected in the highly-polished table tops and cast shadows and pools of pale luminescence across the silk-patterned wallpaper. She could smell the beeswax that shone like glass on the marquetry. Georgiana felt as if she had entered a land of fairy tale and make believe.

A sudden noise drew her attention, and she turned towards a half-open door, through which she could see into a comfortable drawing room. Slowly, she opened the door a little further and noticed that the light in the room came from a five stemmed silver candelabra. No other lights were lit in the room.

It cast a pool of golden warmth across a small table where a young man was seated with a sheaf of papers in one hand and a fine quill pen in the other.

His clothes were fine, yet had the appearance of being slightly worn. His boots had been repaired, and not by a particularly skilful cobbler. His thick, dark hair was a mass of curling, unruly locks, loosely tied at the back with a green twist of silk ribbon that had, undoubtedly, seen better days.

He had not shaved for a day or two, and his cheekbones sported a growth of side whiskers that were too poorly tended to be considered fashionable. He was powerfully built and somehow, intent as he was on the papers he held, reminded Georgiana of a panther preparing to pounce upon its prey. About his badly-shod feet lay a collection of crumpled and hastily discarded sheets. After a moment of absolute stillness, the young man returned to his writing, scribbling with his quill in such haste that he managed to spill droplets of ink upon the table and upon his breeches, although he didn't seem to notice.

Fearful of intruding, yet equally concerned about being rude, having already opened the door somewhat, Georgiana politely coughed, opening the door further.

"Pardon me for intruding, Sir, I trust I am not unduly disturbing you?"

The words hung in the air and the polite question remained unanswered as the young man did not even pause or look up from his notes. Georgiana coughed once more in an attempt to draw his attention.

"My name is Lady Georgiana Branley and, although we have not been formally introduced, I would count it an honour, Sir, to make your acquaintance."

"What?"

Without looking up from his papers, the young man furiously crushed the sheet into a tightly-wadded ball and threw it onto the floor, exclaiming as he did so.

"Damn them! Damn them all to the fiery pits of hell!"

Shocked by the unexpected outburst of profanity, Georgiana gasped and turned on her heel to leave.

"Well! By my faith. If Papa had been alive to hear such a jackanapes speak so roughly, he would have had him thrown from the house for his wretched impudence!"

Part of her was almost tempted to find a jug of water to douse the rude young man's fiery outburst. She was shocked, completely unused to such coarse language, and bewildered that such a crude specimen could be entertained within the walls of the Duke's elegant household. She slammed the door behind her, determined to ignore the oaf and put the unfortunate episode behind her.

Halfway along the corridor, she came upon an open space, a domed gallery that enjoyed windows which would illuminate the chamber with the sun's rays during daylight hours. At night, the room was lit by tall candles. And perfectly placed upon a small, elegant, eight-sided table in the centre of the room was a magnificent chess set, the pieces carved from ivory and ebony, the figures dressed as oriental warriors and fabulously detailed.

Georgiana was instantly bewitched. She had never seen such a beautiful set of chess pieces. Prompted by her insatiable curiosity, she reached towards one of the figures. The cool, smoothness of the beautifully carved ivory took her breath away. Such craftsmanship. The set must have cost a sultan's ransom. The black and white chess board had also been made from an inlay of the finest ivory and ebony - its highly-polished surface provided a wonderful mirror that reflected the figures that stood, ready for battle, upon its perfect surface.

She moved a white pawn and thought about the endless possibilities that the game offered.

A gentle cough startled her and she raised her eyes to see the Duke standing quietly on the other side of the table, watching her carefully.

"Good evening. I trust I didn't startle you. Are you interested in chess, my girl? I could teach you to play, if you were willing."

Georgiana nodded and added a small curtsey as she gestured towards the chess set.

"I've never seen such a beautiful set, Your Grace, and I have learned to play a little already."

The Duke laughed and threw back his head in delight.

"Then may I tempt you, perhaps, to honour me this evening with a game? I see you've already made the first move. Let us play and see if I may assist you in learning a little more."

There were no chairs to seat the players, and the space had been designed to permit onlookers to watch the game. Perhaps even to place a wager on the outcome. Georgiana's opening moves took the Duke a little by surprise.

"You have, perhaps, a disadvantage, my girl, for it has been my experience that members of the fairer sex rarely win at games of war and strategy – certainly most of those of my acquaintance have no skill with such things. I hope it will not end for you too soon!"

"Your Grace, may I ask you a question?"

"Of course, my girl. You may ask me whatever you please."

Despite his bluff bravado, the Duke was having a little difficulty following Georgiana's moves – secretly he was pleased – a challenge was good for the mind, he knew that he played chess fairly well, but he was certainly not an expert. He was, however, definitely not going to admit, to this slip of a girl, that she was making him think hard. Georgiana moved her King's bishop and the Duke frowned.

"I should very much like to return to Casterfield Grange and take up my responsibilities managing my inheritance."

"What? Oh, erm, yes. I mean No, my girl!" The Duke had been caught by surprise, the question not what he had expected at all, whilst his mind was fully engaged by the chess game. He looked up from the game and fixed his gaze on Georgiana.

"What on earth are you asking? I cannot possibly support you in that! I promised your father that I would do all in my power to protect you. That means making sure that you have a fine husband to look after you, a suitable gentleman - a man of means who will be fit and capable to run the estate. You cannot possibly do that on your own. It would be quite unthinkable. And your fortunes would be considerably enhanced by the right marriage. Now, let's have no more talk of you running back to Casterfield Grange, eh?"

Georgiana moved another piece and the Duke chewed on his lower lip and stroked his chin.

"Actually, your Grace, in truth, the house and the lands are mine. I am only claiming what is rightfully mine."

"No, no, no, my girl. They come to you once you're married and not a day before. Until then, they are held by me, in trust for you. You're my guest and I want you to be happy here for as long as you stay. I hope you'll soon meet a gentleman to suit you, and all of this fuss will cease to be of any import. That's my final word on the matter."

The Duke's hand floated above the board, unsure which piece to move, to counter Georgiana's subtle attack. Was it beginner's luck?

"Aha!" he exclaimed. "Now I have you! Check, my girl." He smiled, with a look of relief on his face. "So, who taught you the basics of the game, eh? Must've been a very clever man indeed to have shown you how to play so well. You have done well for a novice."

Georgiana smiled.

"It was a woman, Your Grace. Miss Millpost, in fact. It was she who taught me to play."

The Duke looked up, startled at this statement. He would have to reconsider his opinion of Miss Millpost, in light of this information. It seems that she was full of surprises. He began to understand why old Tillingford had kept her around for so many years.

Georgiana reached forwards and moved a piece.

"Checkmate, Your Grace. Thank you kindly for the game. Perhaps you will permit me to play again so that I may learn some more." She curtsied briefly. "I shall look forward to seeing Your Grace at dinner."

She turned on her heel and walked back down the corridor, a slim and elegant silhouette almost lost amongst the flickering shadows cast by the candlelight. The Duke stared hard at the board and shook his head, scratching his chin and muttering to himself in utter disbelief.

It seemed that Lady Georgiana was also full of surprises. The young girl she had seemed when he first met her, a year before, had matured into a young woman of even stronger character and opinions. He despaired of finding a man that she would choose to marry – he suspected that she was considerably more intelligent than all of them. Perhaps, unpleasant thought, he really might end up having to force the issue.

Chapter Three

A beautifully inlaid long-case clock chimed the hour as Georgiana again made her way along the corridor that led to the marble-floored reception area. She asked a footman to direct her to the dining room, and he responded with a deferential nod before leading her along a broad and exquisitely decorated hallway that opened out into an oak-panelled dining room which shimmered with crystal and candlelight. The dining table was almost fully occupied and she immediately noticed that she and her sister, and Miss Millpost, were the only Ladies present -a most unusual circumstance. Her sister and the Duke were already seated and Cordelia beamed with happiness as Georgiana entered the room. The Duke stood, gallant as ever, to greet his guest. Twenty young men rose as well, all correct politeness.

"Welcome, my girl. You're uncommonly timely for a member of the fairer sex! What other surprises do you have in store for us, eh?" He laughed at his own attempt at humour, mentally cursing his clumsy attempt to lighten the mood.

This young woman was so much harder for him to relate to than her sister! But he would persist, he would honour her father's last wishes and find her a husband, somehow. Georgiana nodded her head politely and smiled at her sister.

"Nothing, I trust, that could spoil your appetite, your Grace."

The Duke nodded and ushered her to a cushioned chair next to his position at the head of the table.

"Two beautiful blooms to grace our table!" he declared to the assembled guests.

As she passed, Georgiana bent to kiss her sister and whispered - "A thorn between two roses?"

Cordelia giggled behind a gloved hand and gave Georgiana a reproving look that urged her to be on her best behaviour.

The Duke stood at the head of the table and made a formal introduction to the assembly, announcing Cordelia as his bride-to-be and the future Duchess of Rotherhithe. He turned with a dramatic gesture and nodded to Georgiana.

"Gentlemen. Can beauty confound the laws of nature and deliver two such wonders from the same line? Evidently, dear friends, lightning has conspired to strike twice in the same place for I am honoured to present to you Lady Georgiana Branley, not only beautiful, but a significant heiress in her own right."

Georgiana was acutely aware of a good twenty young men standing around the table, unable to sit until she did, each one appraising her as if she were a piece of livestock at a cattle auction. Despite her best intentions, she found herself blushing and cast her gaze down, to stare at the silver cutlery set before her.

"Please, Lady Georgiana, be seated – let us be comfortable."

Relieved at the Duke's words, Georgiana settled into her chair. The Duke proceeded to introduce each man in turn and, as each name was called, the gentleman again rose from his seat and bowed formally towards Georgiana. These were her erstwhile suitors, the noble youth of half a dozen counties, all intent on pressing their eligibility and claiming her hand in marriage - and in claiming the wealth to be gained from the rich lands of her estate.

As each man stood and bowed, Georgiana took a little time to appraise them in turn. Some were exceedingly handsome and dressed in the latest fashion. Some of them were quite plain and one had such ravaged skin that Georgiana found it hard to look at him for more than a few moments. And, finally the Duke looked down the length of the grand dining table and announced Oliver, Marquess of Dartworth. To her surprise and discomfort, Georgiana recognised the exceedingly rude young man who had, in the drawing room earlier, shocked her with his appalling manners.

He was sitting at the end of the table where there was less light from the candles, and took a long moment before responding to the Duke's summons to rise and be recognised. So, thought Georgiana, my uncouth jackanapes is a Marquess, is he? He looked even more powerfully built as he rose to his full height, his shoulders broad and strong and his waist narrow above graceful legs. Georgiana couldn't help noticing that he really was, by far, the most handsome man at the table. He bowed politely to Georgiana, but failed to show the slightest hint of recognition.

As the young Marquess resumed his seat, the Duke gestured to the waiting servants to bring in the steaming soup tureens, and the dinner service began. Philip Canterwood, Duke of Rotherhithe, was justifiably proud of his wine cellar and took great delight in entertaining his guests with a selection of very fine vintages. Some of the treasured bottles had been laid down by his father and his grandfather before him. The Duke's hospitality was legendary and his liveried serving men were soon filling fine silver goblets and hand-chased lead crystal glasses with surprisingly potent wines that loosened tongues and led to lively debate amongst the guests.

A heated discussion soon dominated the conversation between the young nobles and the Duke listened with an air of rather paternal indulgence as the guests' voices became louder and the conversation more animated. It seemed that Oliver, Marquess of Dartworth, was but a few years returned from the colonies with tales of the American Constitution and their concept of the rights of the common man. There were some young aristocrats around the table who firmly believed that American independence was an unnatural and wholly undesirable state of affairs.

"My father says that if we hadn't been fighting Bonaparte and the French, we would never have lost the Americas."

Oliver nodded and agreed.

"It's perfectly reasonable to assume that the Crown fought at a disadvantage, but the former colonies have proved themselves more than capable of self-governance. And that's an example that perhaps this great land could learn something from."

"Treasonous rebellion and sedition, Sir!" shouted a man with a high-pitched voice and an almost complete lack of a chin.

"Aye, Sir. You would turn the world upside down and replace order with chaos." Another spoke up, looking offended at the very concept.

Oliver smiled, showing his even white teeth.

"Gentlemen, nothing prevails forever and it is plain to see that the American alternative is not without merit."

"But you would hand over power to the common people and then where would we be?"

Oliver raised a hand and showed the callouses and hard skin that revealed hard toil in the fields.

"As you may know, gentlemen, my late father died, leaving me barely more than his debts as a legacy. Before his death, all he cared for was gambling, hunting and spending money that should have gone to running his estates. When I spoke of that, he simply cut me off. As a result, for some years, until the beginning of hostilities with America caused me to return to England, I ran a plantation in Virginia and was obliged to pay my way with my labours as well as my skills. I can assure you that the experience was far from fatal to my constitution and that I learned much about the principles of freedom and political expression. As I say, we have much to learn from the American example, even if only to protect ourselves from rebellion in the future."

The voices were becoming more animated and the son of a Viscount swung his arm so violently that he spilled his goblet of wine across the damask tablecloth.

"Gentlemen!" The voice of the Duke rang out across the room. "Whilst I encourage discussion and a free exchange of views, we need to be mindful of our manners and exercise some measure of courtesy at this table. This is not the kind of discussion which is suitable for young Ladies!"

The Duke turned to Cordelia, and then Georgiana, his expression rueful. He noted that Miss Millpost had been following the debate with interest, and wondered what she actually thought. The assembled nobles became quiet.

"Our young guest, the Marquess of Dartworth," the Duke raised a manicured hand towards the young man, "may be possessed of some highly unorthodox political notions, but you'll note that he does not raise his voice to enforce his argument."

He let the message sink in for a moment before resuming his conversation with Cordelia.

Despite his earlier rudeness, Georgiana found herself agreeing with the handsome, yet impoverished, young Marquess. She discovered herself to be staring at him, which was rude of her, but she somehow could not bring herself to look away. As conversation resumed, he looked at her down the long length of the table, and Georgiana had the distinct impression that he was really seeing her for the first time. She couldn't be entirely sure, but she thought that he was smiling at her. Not with his mouth, but with his eyes. The look only lasted a few moments and Georgiana had the feeling that, for those precious instants, her heart had stopped beating. It was only him looking away that released her to turn her attention back to food. She felt oddly flushed and a little overheated all of a sudden.

~~~~~

Oliver breathed a quiet sigh of relief when the Duke interrupted the rapidly escalating conversation. Really, he should know better by now. All of these young fops had been raised in the lap of luxury, heirs to titles, protected, by their own status as heirs, from the war that had swallowed their younger siblings. They had been fed traditional views along with their daily food from the time they were babes. They were, simply, not equipped to consider the world any other way.

It was not that he was against the *ton*, and their world of privilege, after all, he was a part of it, even if his father had exemplified the worst of it. He would not, in a fit of revolutionary fervour, throw away his title and abandon those tenants and others who relied on him – although it seemed that was what all of these men expected he was going to do.

He should learn to stay silent – he could better bring change by repairing his father's misdeeds and giving his tenants a better life in the process. That way, the estates would become profitable again, and everyone would benefit, not just him.

The other men turned their attention back to food, obedient to the Duke's wishes, but still muttering under their breath, as if he couldn't hear them! Oliver looked up and discovered that Lady Georgiana was looking straight at him. Their eyes met, and, in an instant, he was lost, the room fading away around him.

Her eyes were a deep blue green, like the sea near the shallows in the tropics, with the sun shining through it. They sparkled in the bright candlelight, watching him with interest, but no apparent condemnation.
~~~~~

That was a new experience. Most people of the nobility, confronted with his opinions on learning from other forms of governing, rapidly expressed, directly or indirectly, disgust, condemnation or revulsion. Yet Lady Georgiana showed no sign of doing so – unlike the gentlemen around him.

It was all the more startling when he remembered, with a flush of embarrassment, that moment when he had been dealing with utter frustration and she had arrived at the door just in time to hear him cursing most inappropriately. She had left before he'd had an opportunity to apologise.

It made her intriguing.

She was beautiful, her soft blonde hair piled up on her head, tendrils escaping to caress her cheek and neck, her skin lightly flushed, her figure the kind that men dream of.

She was the sort of girl that could choose whoever she wanted, with beauty, breeding and money behind her. The sort of girl who wouldn't normally give an impoverished Marquess a second glance. Yet here she was staring into his eyes, quite as intensely as he was staring into hers.

He wanted to know more about her. He wanted, for the first time in a very long time, to be in a position to have something to offer a woman – something beyond a title and a ramshackle collection of poorly maintained estates.

He dragged his eyes away from her, laughing at himself mentally – what sort of fool was he, to be mooning over the woman that all of these men were here to woo, when he couldn't even afford new clothes, let alone anything a woman might want?

But he could still feel her eyes upon him – warm, non-judgemental, interested… he would treasure the memory of that feeling, even if he never felt it again.

~~~~~

Even though Oliver Kentworthy was very much alone in his views, the young Marquess conducted himself with commendable restraint and exemplary manners. If his father had gambled away the family fortune and left the Dartworth estate in a parlous state, Oliver Kentworthy had shown himself well able to rise to the challenge and capable of doing whatever was necessary to support himself. Georgiana was secretly surprised that she found those qualities of independence and initiative more appealing than the wealth and titles that were on offer at this banquet of possible bridegrooms.

At length, the Duke rose from his seat and invited his guests to join him in the library. Whilst it was not usual for the gentlemen and ladies to leave the dining room together, with so few ladies present, the Duke had decided that all of the gentlemen retiring for port and abandoning them would be rather rude. Not to mention the loss of an opportunity for Georgiana to start to get to know some of them. He was, however, a little concerned at the amount of wine that some of his guests had already consumed. He wanted them to present well to young Lady Georgiana, after all! Two footmen opened the library doors as the guests approached and a roaring log fire cast its warmth upon the room.

There was some rather unseemly, and poorly hidden, scuffling and pushing as the gentlemen jockeyed for position, each one trying to sit as close to Georgiana as possible.
~~~~~

With some firm guidance from the Duke and the assistance of a pair of burly footmen in adjusting the placement of chairs, the guests were finally seated and Cordelia graciously accepted her future husband's invitation to play the piano. A natural musician, she played with grace and charm and the room soon stood to applaud and cheer her performance.

The Duke smiled, enjoying the opportunity to bask in the glow of his young bride's accomplishments. She smiled at him, acknowledging that her playing had been intended for his pleasure. Georgiana found the moment quite charming and applauded her sister's delightful interpretation of a difficult classical piece.

The Duke turned to Georgiana and asked if she would be kind enough to offer the assembly a sample of her musical talents. Georgiana blushed as she smiled.

"Your Grace, I must confess that I am completely without the least shred of ability and have never studied the musical arts. Fortunately, my dear sister has more than enough talent for the two of us."

The Duke frowned in disappointment.

"You do not play an instrument, my girl? But it is such a fundamental feminine accomplishment!"

"I am afraid, your Grace, that I do not."

"Clearly, you might have profited from more study of music as well as the usually masculine pursuit of chess." Miss Millpost, unnoticed by the Duke, pursed her lips, her eyes narrowed in annoyance at this sad demonstration of the predictable male perspective. She sighed.

"I am sure that Your Grace is perfectly correct," Georgiana replied, with her eyes downcast, "but I fear it is probably far too late to remedy my shortcomings in the musical arts. Cordelia has been playing since she was a small child."

The Duke was evidently not pleased with her reply.

"In the light of Lady Georgiana's wishes, do we have any volunteers in the room who might aspire to offer us a tune or two?"

The moment passed and two gentlemen stood up simultaneously to take the seat at the piano. There was another bout of unseemly posturing as the men competed for the small stool.

"Gentlemen!" The Duke's voice rang out and the two men ceased their inelegant struggle. "I had hoped for musical entertainment on the pianoforte. Not a bout of musical chairs!"

The room erupted into laughter and one of the gentlemen reluctantly relinquished the struggle and left the piano in the hands of a notably talented player. Soon the soothing notes were filling the room with an exquisite sense of melancholy as the young man played and sang a popular ballad of unrequited love, and the room joined in with the familiar chorus. He had a fine voice and the assembly showed its enthusiasm by calling for more. He bowed to the Duke and happily complied.

Evidently, the Duke had quickly forgotten about Georgiana's failure to offer any kind of musical entertainment. Most of the young gentlemen then took turns either at the pianoforte or reciting poetry. Not all of them shared the same level of artistic expression as the first, but the entertainment was pleasing and delightfully distracting.

It was eventually noticed, however, that the Marquess of Dartworth was less than enthusiastic about offering his talents as an entertainer. The other young nobles, clearly unhappy with his unconventional political views, goaded him and accused him of being tone deaf, and afraid to advertise his lack of ability.

The Marquess silently rose and took up his place at the piano, the others making snide remarks behind their hands at the poor state of his clothing and boots. Oliver Kentworthy ignored them all. He brushed a curling lock of hair back from his forehead and closed his eyes. The room became quiet with anticipation. He lifted his chin and began to sing in a pure, resonant baritone that sent shivers down Georgiana' spine. His voice was pure and strong, smooth and sweet like dripping honey and the room was mesmerised by his words.

He sang a ballad he'd learned in the Colonies, a tale of love and loss about two people whose paths crossed for one night before they were separated forever. He finished the song, his eyes still closed, and only the crackle of the fire broke the silence. Georgiana, entranced, and fascinated by this man, who seemed such a bundle of contradictory skills, ideas and attitudes, discovered, to her amazement, that there was a tear, sneaking its way from the corner of her eye. She brushed it away as the Duke coughed to break the spell.

"Well, that's enough of melancholy tales for one evening! Let us have something a little more cheerful to end the day on a happier note."

He called the first player to the piano, to lend his gifts once more, and the crowd soon forgot Oliver's haunting tale of bittersweet sadness as they cheered and chorused a rousing country song that raised their spirits and dispelled the gloom.

~~~~~

As the guests departed to find their bedchambers and sleep off the excess of wine that had sparked such lively discussions over dinner, Cordelia took Georgiana's hand and suggested that they walk together to Georgiana's sumptuous quarters.

"We need to speak, Georgiana, and preferably behind closed doors."

The chambermaid had built a merry fire in the grate and the room was lit by slender candles that cast a warm glow over the richly woven Persian rugs.

The sisters sat comfortably next to the fire and Cordelia began by eagerly describing the young men who'd attended the banquet.

"If I were not betrothed to the Duke, I am sure I would be spoiled for choice by so many fine and handsome young men! Tell me, Georgie – which one did you like the most? Or are you interested in two or three or more of them?"

Georgiana paused before speaking.

"My darling sister, I know how much you enjoy these banquets, which is just as well, because you'll be entertaining the Duke's friends and guests whenever the occasion arises. But I have to confess that I found the evening to be a bit of a bore. I really don't like any of them much – they did nothing to impress me, nothing at all!"

Cordelia drew in her breath in shock.

"A bit of a bore? Georgiana! You surely cannot mean that."
~~~~~

Her sister nodded her head in assent and wrung her hands in frustration.

"My only desire is to get back to Casterfield Grange and see that the estate is being properly run," she replied. "I'm not very fond of these social affairs and I can't play an instrument. Cordelia, you know full well that I can barely put one foot in front of another on the dance floor. I'm hopeless on these grand occasions."

"But there were so many handsome young men at the table and every one of them would willingly give an arm to claim you as his bride."

Georgiana laughed.

"To claim me, surely, and the lands I hold."

There was a note of cynicism in Georgiana's voice and there was also a hint of desperation. Cordelia frowned, worried.

"My beloved sister, you know you will have to choose one of them. You must marry. It's as simple as that. I have been most fortunate in Papa's choice of a husband. Now you must choose someone for yourself and you will have to make that choice very soon."

Georgiana sighed. "I know. I know."

But she didn't sound very convinced. A silence settled between the two young women as they were lost in their private thoughts.

"Georgiana, let us speak plainly with one another. I know who I would choose if I were in your shoes. Now tell me which of the suitors caught your eye?"

"Well, to be truthful, as I said before, I found all of them spectacularly boring."

Cordelia shook her head in disbelief.

"Except perhaps for the man who sang the lament so beautifully at the end of the evening."

"The ragged man? Oh, Georgiana. Surely not him?"

"Well, you did ask me, you insisted I give you some kind of answer, and you wanted me to speak plainly. He is the only one who was remotely interesting."

"Oliver Kentworthy? The poorest man in the room? The one they refer to as the revolutionary from the Colonies? Please tell me that you're not serious, Georgiana!"

"You must admit he's handsome. And he's a man of principles. It's quite clear that he has a caring nature and I find that, well, interesting." Georgian felt herself blush as she spoke. It occurred to her that she had never said anything so flattering about a man before. But then, she had never actually found any man remotely interesting before.

Now it was Cordelia's turn to wring her hands.

"But he's a brute! He's worked with his hands like some common labourer. And his silly ideas betray a complete lack of intelligence. No, my darling sister, you can do so much better than a poorly shod carthorse from the shire. There are thoroughbreds aplenty on hand, men of wealth and means and power."

Georgiana lowered her head to avoid looking at her sister, as Cordelia continued to speak.

"Sleep on it and we will speak on the matter again tomorrow. Perhaps some common sense will find its way into that wayward head of yours!" Despite her concerns, Cordelia smiled at her sister and reached forward to take her hands. "We only want what is best for you, Georgiana."

She leaned closer to kiss her sister's forehead, before rising from her chair and bidding her sister a peaceful and good night's sleep. She turned to make her way to her own bedchamber, hoping that she had managed to dissuade Georgiana from her first, and obviously disastrous, choice of a potential future husband.

But as she made her way along the candlelit corridor, she was far from convinced that she had succeeded.

Chapter Four

To her surprise, Georgiana slept deeply in her comfortable four-poster bed and was woken by the chirruping of early morning birdsong and by a smiling chambermaid who curtsied in the doorway and asked permission to make up the fire and bring a basin of hot water. The Duke was hosting a large number of guests and the servants were busy long before the first hint of dawn lit up the sky. Georgiana breathed deeply and smelled a delicious hint of fresh baked bread from the kitchens. She nodded to the maid with a smile and enjoyed the warm cosiness of her comfortable bed for a few minutes more.

Rising from her woollen blankets, Georgiana washed herself in the privacy of her chambers and thought about the dreams that had come to her during the peaceful hours of the night. She recalled a particularly vivid dream where she was riding a powerful, black stallion with a long, flowing mane, clinging to its back as it vaulted over hedgerows and galloped across the countryside.

It was so exhilarating, so vivid, the warmth of its sides against her legs as she gripped so tightly to avoid falling.

'I wonder who my black stallion might be in this great household of thoroughbreds!' she pondered, as she dressed for breakfast. The thought made her smile, yet she was deeply perturbed by the fact that she was expected to pick a husband within the next few weeks and surrender herself to a marriage without even having the chance to get to know her future husband much.

It was absurd, but Cordelia had hinted that if she did not make her mind up soon, before Cordelia's wedding, the Duke would take it upon himself to choose someone for her. It was a monstrous proposition and Georgiana felt powerless in the face of such relentless pressure. *'At least you can sell or exchange a horse. With husbands, it's an altogether trickier situation!'* She thought as she placed an embroidered and perfumed kerchief in her sleeve and made her way down to the spacious dining room for breakfast.

Some of the gentlemen guests were still nursing their hangovers after a surfeit of fine wine the evening before. The conversation was calmer and more muted as the servants hurried from place to place with freshly baked rolls and salted butter, damson preserves and honey, cold, cured meats and boiled eggs. Last to arrive at the dining table was Oliver Kentworthy, looking completely fresh and free of any hint of a hangover. He had shaved that morning, and the faint blue hue of his shaved whiskers lent a pleasing contrast to his tanned features. Georgiana smiled as he took his place and he nodded to her in acknowledgement, the smile extending this time from his blue eyes all the way to his mouth.

Georgiana felt warmed by that smile, as if it had somehow touched her like the sun coming from behind a cloud. Flustered, she forced herself to concentrate on breakfast, unsure, suddenly, of how to go on.

The coffee was excellent, prepared by a Spanish servant who had learned the art in distant Cuba, and everyone congratulated the Duke on his wonderful hospitality. The Duke smiled at his guests, always pleased to note that his table presented some of the finest dishes in the county, and possibly much further beyond.

Georgiana asked him how the coffee was prepared, that it became be so wonderfully flavoursome and frothy. It was the first time that she had ever tasted coffee that had been made in this fashion.

"Hah! It should be a state secret, my girl. Can't have everyone stealing the secrets of my kitchens, can we?" He laughed and called one of the servants to the table. "Please explain to the Lady how the coffee is prepared, Julio."

The man nodded and seemed to enjoy sharing the details of how the finely ground beans were added to boiling water before they were squeezed through layers of the finest muslin, which separated the grounds so that the beverage arrived with a delicious layer of foam atop the cup.

"In faith, Your Grace, I should dearly love to try my hand at making coffee in such a novel fashion."

"Heavens, no, my girl. We can't have you ruining your pretty hands doing the work of kitchen maids, can we? Whatever would the world be coming to?"

The Duke looked down the table at Oliver Kentworthy and drew in a quiet breath. He found himself profoundly disturbed by the young Marquess. The man's father had been a wastrel, that was true, and Oliver was to be respected for surviving regardless, and not following in those disgraceful footsteps. But... to have done manual labour, to have mixed freely with the common men in the fields, even when bearing the role of the manager of an estate – that was a concept he found challenging. How would the world go on, if no-one knew their place in the fabric of society?

"We need to remember our place in the world and maintain our standards and our dignity, Georgiana. We can't all abandon our positions and toil as common field hands. That would never do." Mentally Philip winced, as he heard how harsh his own words sounded. Too late, it was spoken.

Oliver looked up from his bone china breakfast plate and moved a sliver of cold beef into his mouth, his eyes on the Duke, coolly appraising the great aristocrat and assessing his quietly spoken comments. The Duke looked away first, too uncomfortable to hold the young Marquess' piercing gaze. He called for more coffee and some of the sleepier guests began to revive their spirits as the finely ground beans worked their magic and chased away the shadows of the previous evening's drinking.

A lively conversation sprang up about who owned the fastest horse for point to point racing, a source of immense pride and competition amongst the local gentry. Oliver's indifference to the subject marked him, yet again, as an outsider, a man without money or means.

As someone who simply didn't belong amongst the privileged young aristocrats who were enjoying the Duke's lavish hospitality. Yet it was evident that he was completely indifferent to the stares and slights that were occasionally directed at him. He seemed to inhabit his own private world and, as Georgiana watched him from her end of the table, she began to wonder what on earth this exceptionally handsome young man was doing at the Duke's house in the first place.

As the servants cleared away the plates from the hearty breakfast, Cordelia took Georgiana's hand and suggested that they go for a walk in the gardens to get some fresh air. Georgiana's face lit up at the prospect. It was an uncommonly sunny day and the frost was quickly melting on the new spring grass.

"Wrap up warmly and we can explore the grounds around the house. I know how much you love the plants and flowers, but you must solemnly promise not to get down on your hands and knees and start weeding, or Philip will have an apoplexy!"

The sisters laughed at the thought and Georgiana hurried to her chambers to find suitable clothes, and her fur muff to keep her hands warm in the cool, morning air.

It was such a relief to be out in the fresh air, the pale sunlight warming her face and birds singing in the trees. It reminded her so much of her beloved home and how much she missed being in her own familiar house. The two sisters linked arms and strolled along the perfectly swept pathways that led through the gardens. It was a wonderful interlude, a private moment that allowed the young Ladies to talk without fear of being overheard.

"Georgiana, with the benefit of a good night's sleep, have you thought any more about your future husband?"

"Not really. It's just so difficult. I feel like that queen in the Greek legends who was surrounded by suitors who pressed her, every day, for an answer. I can't just close my eyes and pick one at random."

"Queen Penelope, the faithful wife of Ulysses. That's who you're referring to, isn't it? See, I know something of the classics too!" They laughed. "She waited twenty years for her husband to return, Georgie, my dear. But you only have a few weeks to make up your mind."

They walked a little further in silence, each young woman lost in her private thoughts and, as they turned a corner marked by a row of perfectly clipped decorative bushes, they almost bumped into the Duke. He was not alone. At his side stood the imposing figure of the Marquess of Dartworth. The Duke doffed his elegant hat, stepped forward and placed a chaste kiss upon his future wife's cheek and then turned and bent to kiss Georgiana's hand. Oliver bowed formally to both Ladies.

After a moment, the Duke exclaimed "My dear, it is most fortunate that we have met here, for I have just recalled that I have a number of pressing issues to discuss with you concerning the wedding. With this many guests in the house, I would like to seize this chance for quiet conversation whilst I may."

The Duke turned to Oliver and nodded. "Pray excuse us whilst we attend to these important matters, Dartworth. May I take my leave of you, and trust you to take care of Lady Georgiana in my absence? I will send one of the maids to follow you at a distance, for proprieties sake."

Oliver bowed to the Duke and tried to conceal a smile that almost threatened to break into open laughter.

"Certainly, you may, Your Grace."

Philip and his future wife walked at a leisurely pace, arm in arm, back towards the great house. Oliver was still smiling.

"Well, my Lady, I hope that you are appreciative of the dramatic arts, for I fear we have just witnessed an extraordinary act of theatre."

Georgiana raised a hand to her mouth as she laughed out loud.

"'Tis true, my Lord, that I am an admirer of the arts, but I confess that I have seen much better performances in my time."

They both laughed at the contrived meeting.

"I daresay my good sister had a hand in this charade, for we have been well and truly forced upon one another, and I would pray that my presence is not a burden upon your good nature, my Lord."

"My name is Oliver, my Lady, and I would count it an honour if you would address me by that name. I have become accustomed to life with less formality."

Georgiana smiled.

"I am Georgiana and, as we have been officially introduced, I am quite amenable to dispensing with some of the formalities."

Oliver bowed in an exaggerated impersonation of a courtier sweeping his hat low before his queen.

"Your devoted servant, my Lady."

Georgiana couldn't stop herself from laughing out loud.

"Why sir, though a Marquess, I do declare that you have something of the circus in your veins!"

"I fear there are clowns enough in this great house without my adding to the company of fools."

"Oliver, would you care to walk with me? I see Mary hovering on the path, and I am certain that she will ensure that we are properly chaperoned, without intruding upon our privacy."

"The pleasure would be mine, Georgiana."

They adopted a formal distance between them the hand resting lightly on his arm, their manner all that propriety could require, and, taking this opportunity to converse in private, they found that they could talk quite freely. For each of them, there was an instant sense of comfort with the other, as if they had known each other for years, rather than having only just met.

"Oliver, may I ask you a question?"

The Marquess nodded his assent with a ready smile, and it was perfectly obvious that he was enjoying Georgiana's company far more than she had originally expected he would, given the way that she had been foisted upon him by her sister and the Duke.

"When first I saw you yesterday evening, seated with pen and paper in the drawing room, I addressed you and you completely ignored me. Pray tell me, why was that?"

Oliver stopped for a moment and turned towards her.

"I can only offer you my most humble apologies, Lady Georgiana. I have no excuse for my rudeness, but I was struggling with a most vexing correspondence and a delicate matter that I have found most troubling."

Georgiana paused in the hope that he would speak further. When he was silent, she felt compelled to reassure him.

"Oliver, I assure you that you could tell me anything, and feel secure in the knowledge that I would always honour your confidence, and never repeat a word to another soul."

The young Marquess pursed his lips, his blue eyes darkening as if storm clouds passed across the sky, and considered Georgiana's words. After a minute's pause, he breathed out heavily in a long sigh, and seemed to have come to a conclusion.

"You have probably already heard much about my circumstances. The rumours have been a popular enough subject for idle salon gossip." He paused, then went on with a sad sigh. "The fact is that my late father squandered the family fortune, and all he has left to me is his title, the barely maintained entailed properties, and a slew of gambling debts. I have paid many of them, but the amount was astounding - five thousand pounds of debt yet remains. The creditors would have all the remaining goods that could be sold, and leave me quite penniless in an empty, crumbling house."

Georgiana said nothing as she absorbed the news, although Oliver had quite openly mentioned his circumstances during dinner, he had not, then gone into detail of just how poor a state his father had left the Marquessate in. They walked further in silence until Georgiana spoke again.

"Oliver, I have not, actually, heard the rumours – I have not been about in society much at all, since my father's death six months ago. I am truly sorry for your troubles. It is not right that a son should pay for his father's folly."

"You are most kind to say so, and you may well be right, but the law would happily leave me penniless. I have been writing to my father's creditors to seek a better answer to his debts. All they want is their coin and they would sell my possessions tomorrow if they could, to cover the debts. It is a most troubling situation."

He turned to face her once more. "So, I am hardly a good candidate as a husband." He lowered his eyes, unwilling to look at her. "In fact, the only reason that I have been invited here is that my father raised enough capital just before he died to pay a wager that he owed to the Duke. In appreciation of his effort, and honourable action in doing so, the Duke promised my father that he would find me a bride. He has made a token gesture by inviting me here, but he surely does not intend to support me in any suit I may press for your hand." He sighed again. "I can only guess that you must be relieved to know that."

Georgiana reached for Oliver's hand, instinctively wanting to comfort him.

"Do not say that, my Lord."

Her touch surprised him, and he looked up into her beautiful blue green eyes and saw only compassion and generosity. And perhaps something more. Or perhaps he was foolishly deluding himself – why would she do more than extend a bare minimum of kindness?

"But I must. I am the most hopeless suitor to attend this house party. I am mocked by the others for my clothing, although I could not care less what they think. Yet I must confess that I would prefer to be a wealthier man, if it would improve my esteem in your eyes."

"You do not need wealth to be a good man, Oliver. And the popinjays who preen and strut about Philip's house are only interested in my lands and dowry, and their pockets. They have no other interest in me. It is most distressing to be compelled to choose a husband from amongst the ranks of such shallow and spineless creatures."

"It seems that Fate has been unkind to us, Georgiana. I would never wish you to think that I saw you only as a source of wealth – I am not that shallow! I may need money more than all of them do, yet I care only for the fact that you are a most interesting and caring person. My circumstances conspire to prevent me from asking for your hand and, even if I did ask, the Duke would reject my offer in favour of another."

"Do you think I would say 'No', Oliver?"

"I would not dare to hope for anything else."

"Yet I took you for a braver man than that."

Silence fell between them, as they walked slowly around the ornamental gardens, the flowers still dormant from the touch of winter and waiting for the growing warmth of springtime to release them from their bondage, the faintest green shoots and leaf buds just becoming visible on the trees. The moment was peaceful, and remarkably pleasant, despite the serious tone of their discussion.

"Oliver, these manoeuvrings from the Duke and his circle of friends are not to my liking. It is like a game of chess where the rules of play are ignored and the outcome is already decided before the first piece is moved."

"That is a perfect description of the situation. Your wishes will not be observed or respected, and your dowry and lands will probably go to the highest bidder, so to speak, or to the man most favoured by the Duke. They will always say that it is in your best interests, but it is only about the value of your estate. And that pains me."

"And why, my Lord, does that pain you?"

"Because there is not an ounce of love or joy or respect in these grubby commercial dealings and I believe that a Lady of your character deserves far better than that."

Once again, the young Marquess had managed to take Georgiana's breath quite away.

"You are too kind, Oliver. But then, pray tell me who I should marry."

"You should be free to choose for yourself, if and when you are truly ready, and not sold off by this forced bloodstock auction that turns my stomach."

"And of the assembled nobles who compete for my hand and my lands, which of them would you favour as my future husband?"

He looked at her and there was a moment when she thought her heart had entirely stopped beating. Her cheeks flushed, and the pale sun was suddenly overly warm.

Her breath came fast and she found herself staring helplessly at his full sensual lips, waiting for the words that would fall from them.

"Why, Georgiana, is the answer not entirely obvious to you?"

"Speak the words, Oliver, and let me understand if my intuition is better schooled than my dancing or musical skills."

"I would nominate myself, if I had the means to support you in the style to which you are accustomed, and which you deserve, dearest Lady Georgiana."

Georgiana drew in a sharp breath, and it seemed as if the birds had stopped singing in the trees whilst time stood completely still.

"But I cannot fulfil my wish, because I am a penniless near vagrant and I am sure that the Duke has already chosen a suitable husband for you. I can only wish that he will make you as happy as I would want to."

A deep, sonorous bell was being rung somewhere inside the house to announce luncheon and, startled at how much time had passed as they walked and spoke, the couple stopped for a moment. Oliver dragged his eyes away from Georgiana, unwillingly, schooling his expression to one of neutral politeness as they turned together to follow the winding pathway that led back to the grand entrance. Servants were already carrying plates of hot food from the kitchen and pouring wine from silver jugs. A fire had been lit in the enormous hearth to keep the room warm and the guests were arriving in twos and threes from their card games and amusements.

As Georgiana took her place at the Duke's side, she was not looking forward to her luncheon. She seemed to have lost her appetite. Her sister smiled at her and Georgiana understood that the meeting with Oliver had been contrived purely to emphasise how unsuitable the young Marquess would be as a suitor.

Whether the ploy had worked was not certain, for Georgiana felt something in her heart that she had never felt before. She suspected that Cordelia would be horrified to discover that, perhaps, the ploy had created quite the opposite effect from that intended.

For, whilst she couldn't be absolutely certain, Georgiana feared that she was feeling the first stirrings of a deep and powerful attraction that threatened to overwhelm her. She liked Oliver. She liked his honesty, his plain speaking, the fact that he seemed to actually see her as an independent person, capable of thinking for herself. She felt strange in his presence – but in a good way. She found that she wanted to spend more time in his company, not less. She glanced up at where he sat, so far off down the table, his face a picture of artificial calm, and wanted to cry. She was not a girl who cried easily, or often – so this was a truly odd experience.

She raised a lace napkin to her mouth but used the embroidered corner to dab away a small tear that had appeared at the corner of her eye. She did not know why, but in the midst of the feasting and merrymaking, the joyful approach of Cordelia and Philip's wedding, she felt, in that instant, ready to sob her heart out. As soon as possible, she excused herself from the table, and took herself to her room.

Chapter Five

The evenings drew in quickly as the last frosts of winter faded before the first hints of spring. The great house was illuminated by rows and rows of flickering candles and servants hurried to make sure that all of the rooms were well lit by a forest of glowing flames. Fires were prepared and the warmth of crackling logs spilled a welcome heat into the great halls and salons of the beautifully appointed stately mansion.

Two weeks had passed since their arrival, and Georgiana found each day harder than the one before. As Cordelia's happiness grew, so did Georgiana's misery. The more she saw of the young men that were supposed to be suitable choices as potential husbands, the more revolted she felt. They were all so shallow, so sure in their opinions and their place in the world, with little care for anyone else. They looked at her with greedy eyes, and she felt, even more, like a broodmare at a livestock auction – assessed for her fineness of form but with no attention paid to her character at all.

She had found little opportunity to talk to Oliver – since the staged meeting, the Duke and Cordelia had made sure that she was forced to strictly observe propriety, and Cordelia or Miss Millpost went with her everywhere. They were left with inane snippets of conversation in the drawing room, surrounded by other guests, and moments when their eyes met, and spoke in silence of the sadness they shared.

As the day of Cordelia's wedding approached, more guests arrived – to stay in the house, and to stay at the Inn in the nearby village. Every night, dinner was attended by a much larger gathering of guests than the night before. An extension had been added to the dining table to accommodate more visitors and by eight o'clock the assembled gentry had been suitably refreshed with glasses of dry sherry and sweet madeira.

There were more couples in the house and some of the young bachelors were greeted by their doting parents, who were curious to see if their precious boy was going to be successful and marry into a valuable estate. Georgiana shook her head in disbelief. It was beginning to resemble a cattle auction and she recognised that she was widely regarded as the prize milk cow on offer to the highest bidder.

One particular evening, as the wine flowed and the sumptuous dishes were served, the conversation turned once more to the Marquess of Dartworth's unusual political opinions, and soon the table was dominated by the shouts of outraged parents who saw the young man as a threat to the good order of society. As the official centre of the table's attention, Georgiana, the landed potential bride-in-waiting, was soon consulted on her views. Cordelia groaned quietly and shot a warning glance at her headstrong and independent sister.

"I can only argue from the perspective of reason and logic and I am therefore compelled to agree with the Marquess of Dartworth's assertion that the practice of democracy has achieved extraordinary freedom and prosperity for the citizens of the former Colonies."

There were gasps of outrage and the wizened Duke of Belvoir muttered "But you're only a slip of a girl, for Heaven's sake. What on earth could you possibly know of reason and logic, eh? These are matters that only a man's mind might grasp!"

Georgiana bowed in deference to the aged man's title and replied.

"Your Grace, I beg your forgiveness for confounding the laws of nature and revealing a modest grasp of reason. I did not intend to shock you. I hope you will not be further troubled by any other displays of what I had assumed was nothing more than plain common sense."

The old Duke stuttered and fumbled for a reply but had to satisfy himself with an irritated shake of the head and a deep draught of spiced wine that completely failed to improve his mood. He continued to mumble to himself.

"Girls and reason? Logic? Stuff and nonsense, I tell you. Stuff and nonsense!"

It was clear to everyone that, although Georgiana may have an attractive inheritance to bring to her wedding, she was sadly lacking in the poise, good manners and sense of place that was expected of a woman of the *ton*. The qualities which would make her a good and obedient wife appeared to be lamentably absent.

Cordelia was only too aware of the subdued muttering that was running around the table. Some of the older guests were openly staring at her sister, gaping at her in wonder as if she were an exhibit in a zoo or a freak in a travelling circus. The evening was not going as planned. Cordelia was praying that her sister's headstrong behaviour had not deterred some of the wealthier candidates from pursuing their chances of matrimony. A valuable estate was one thing. A headstrong and independent wife was an abomination in the minds of many of the assembled guests.

Though one individual couldn't help smiling at Georgiana's wit and evident spirit. Oliver nodded at her and raised his goblet to signal his admiration. Cordelia noticed the gesture and frowned. This was not how she had intended the evening to proceed. The Duke was drumming his fingers on the white damask tablecloth and looking down the table at Oliver. The young Marquess smiled and raised a silent toast to his host who nodded graciously at the other man, although not with the slightest hint or degree of warmth in his expression.

The dinner concluded with a magnificent pudding, lavishly decorated with a fabulous spun-sugar confection that carried the Duke's coat of arms. Everyone cheered and applauded as the pudding was formally presented to the table and the Duke assumed the honour of carving out the first slice, which he offered, with a bow, to Cordelia. He was greeted with cries of encouragement for his gallant gesture and the delicious confectionary was quickly divided up amongst the guests and consumed with great relish. Georgiana watched them in horrified fascination. They reminded her of pigs at a trough.

As the dinner drew to a close and the servants hurried forward to clear away the dishes, the Duke stood up with Cordelia at his side. When everyone became quiet, he called out to the assembled guests that they were invited to join him and the future Duchess of Rotherhithe in the blue drawing room, to enjoy a hand of cards and, perhaps, a game of chess. He smiled broadly and reminded everyone that it was entirely acceptable for his guests to place wagers on the outcomes, because he had to recover the costs of the dinner in whatever way he could. The guests roared with laughter and followed the Duke and his future bride into the well-lit drawing room.

<p style="text-align:center">~~~~~</p>

Philip watched his laughing guests as they made their way from the dining room, and frowned. He wished that he felt better about all of this. Georgiana had shown no preference for any of the possible candidates for husband – in fact she appeared to have somewhat of an aversion to the majority of them. Except for Dartworth – which was a great worry. He had promised the boy's father that he would help him find a wife, and had thought, at first, that he might have a magical solution to his promises to two dead men, but then he had met Dartworth.

The Marquess was totally unsuitable for Georgiana – he would not be truly fulfilling his promise to Tillingford if he let the girl marry a man who had absolutely no money, even if he did have a title. And the boy had such outrageous opinions – opinions he was fool enough to share. It just wouldn't do.

A pity though – for he suspected that old Tillingford wouldn't have cast aside Oliver's opinions entirely – he had always been very focused on looking after his tenants and encouraging them to have a say in the way the farms were run – and it had worked out well for him. Still you just couldn't go about saying that sort of thing amongst the *ton* and expect to be well received!

And the money – if the boy couldn't sort out the remaining debts fast, he likely would end up in the worst disgrace, and in debtors' prison – not the sort of thing one could accept in the husband of a gently bred Lady.

There was nothing for it – if the boy survived dealing with the debt, he would help him find a bride – but for now, for Georgiana, he would have to choose the best of the available bunch, and convince her, force her hand if necessary, to marry the man. He wouldn't rest easy until he had fulfilled his promise to old Tillingford and the girl was well married and settled.

~~~~~

"Still feeling out of sorts, Otford?"

Baron Setford's voice was quiet, neutral in tone, his face calm as he sipped his brandy appreciatively, leaning back in his chair. The remnants of a surprisingly decent meal scattered the table before them, and the fire crackled in the grate. This inn had turned out to be a good choice as a stop along the way. The private parlour was clean and pleasant, the food and brandy good, and the bedchambers had looked equally well maintained.

Gerald was silent, staring into the fire, deciding if he would answer at all.
~~~~~

Eventually, faced with Setford's patient silence, he spoke.

"Not out-of-sorts exactly. More lost, not to put too fine a point on it."

Setford nodded, pleased with the honesty, and waited for the younger man to continue. Gerald Otford, newly Baron Tillingford, looked up, and his deep blue eyes met Setford's clear grey ones. Those deep blue eyes held a wealth of buried anguish.

"This whole business of having been ennobled… I never expected having a title and estates to come with so much responsibility – and with so much exhausting need to subtly prove to the *ton* that I am worthy of the honour. Hunter's wedding was a classic example of why I'm feeling so lost. It was wonderful to see the other Hounds, and with them, I felt almost comfortable. But… all of those other society people, that massive room full of titles and importance… I had no idea how to deal with it at all!"

"But you did deal with it. And well. You gave them nothing to disdain, you comported yourself better than half of them. And, from what I hear, you are doing a sterling job with the Tillingford estates. So… why is it bothering you today? "

Gerald sipped from his glass, and held eye contact with Setford (not something that many people were comfortable doing).

"Because you are about to drop me into another pool of society gossip and hidden agendas, where I've never even met most of the people who will be there! I feel as much in danger as I did in the field in Spain."

Setford laughed – not mockery, but a sincere appreciation of the analogy.

"You'll do well. Rotherhithe has occasional lapses into being a bit painfully traditional, but he's a good man m'boy. Trust him. Try to enjoy yourself – use this as an opportunity to lurk quietly and observe them all. Learn some more about the upcoming generation of the *ton*. Can't say that many of them impress me, but it will be a good thing to work out who you can trust, and who you'll want to steer clear of."

Gerald laughed in turn, with a rather more brittle edge than Setford.

"Enjoy myself! You are an optimist. But study them – yes, I'll do that. I'd just feel better if some of the other Hounds were there – I feel remarkably exposed without them at my back. No offence to you, sir."

"Damn it m'boy, it's just a wedding and a house party, not a battle. Although..." Setford's sharp grey eyes twinkled with amusement, "...a collection of hopeful young men, with an eye on a sizeable dowry, trying to convince the younger Branley girl that she should choose them, could potentially turn into something resembling a battlefield."

That brought a smile, and a more genuine laugh from Gerald, and he relaxed a little. Whatever happened, the spymaster was a good man to have on your side. He would manage this next few weeks. Setford yawned.

"Time for us to turn in. If we get a good start in the morning, we'll be there before dinner tomorrow."

Chapter Six

The following day went much as most of the recent days had, with a slow start after the evening's drinking, and a scatter of socially acceptable activities, such as walks in the gardens, rides in the grounds, a little hunting for the gentlemen, cards, or embroidery and gossip for the ladies, throughout the day. The late afternoon found all gathered in the main salon for tea and desultory conversation.

As the afternoon sun turned the mist of soft green from the new leaves on the trees to a rich gold, making the view from the salon window quite enchanting, a carriage was heard approaching up the long drive. Cordelia, with her usual curiosity, managed to nonchalantly move to the window to peek out and watch to see who was arriving. Georgiana, thoroughly bored by then, and sick of inane conversation, joined her.

"I wonder who it is? Oh, my, doesn't the park look beautiful in this light? I so miss Casterfield Grange! The buds will be out on all our trees too." Georgiana sighed, still watching the carriage.

Cordelia squinted a bit into the light, trying to see if the carriage bore a crest of any kind. It didn't.

"There is no crest. It could be anyone. We will simply have to wait until they are announced." She went back to watching the progress of the carriage, happy to ignore the ongoing gossip in the room behind her.

As usual, the ladies were talking about the latest scandals, and casting long disapproving looks at some of the gentlemen, especially at the Marquess of Dartworth. The gentlemen were talking about hunting, and, as far as she could tell, about the latest 'men's gossip' around who was courting who, and who was having an affair with who, although they did try to be quiet enough for the ladies not to hear. They, also, were casting negative looks at Oliver, and excluding him from their conversation.

Georgiana wanted to scream. She would have been so much better off at home, working with the estate manager, caring for her lands and tenants, rather than here, a prize on display. They were all fools. The only interesting person here was Oliver. And she knew that both Cordelia and Philip disapproved of him.

She wondered how Philip had ever brought himself to even invite Oliver. Seeing how everyone treated Oliver made her grind her teeth, wanting to shout at them about how rude they were. Two years ago, she might have done just that. Now, she was trying very hard to be a polite young Lady. It was, perhaps, the most difficult thing she had ever done.

Her heart went out to him, watching how he dealt with it all, with quiet dignity.

The sound of the carriage wheels on the gravel at the entry brought her out of her thoughts.

Moments later, the butler knocked, opened the salon doors and announced – "Baron Sefton, and Baron Tillingford."

Georgiana and Cordelia both started – they still struggled to adjust to the fact that someone else now bore the title that had been their father's. After a deep breath, they both smiled, and went forward to greet the handsome gentleman who stood in the doorway, looking a little nervous as Philip welcomed him.

They had met Gerald Otford only once before, just a few months ago. They liked him – for once, the sisters were in complete agreement. Georgiana particularly liked him, because he had listened to her, respected her ideas and knowledge of estate management, and generally treated her as an adult with thoughts worth hearing. She was glad that he had come – between him, and Setford, she at least had a chance of more decent conversation!

As they were announced, a hush had fallen in the room, as everyone assessed the newcomers. Setford was well known, even if he did not go about in society much. He had vast influence, and was treated with careful respect. The new Baron Tillingford was another matter entirely. He was recently raised to his title, and, whilst coming from a respectable landed gentry family, was seen by most of the *ton* as an upstart. They just hadn't found anything yet to denigrate him for. And, well, he was wealthy, and he was a war hero, and handsome. In the eyes of the *ton's* mamas, that forgave a lot.

The men eyed him, wondering if he was another competitor for Georgiana's hand.

Georgiana was certain that he wasn't anything like that. He was, amongst a horde of people who didn't care, a friend.

∿∿∿∿∿

As the carriage rolled up the long drive of Canterwood Park, Gerald looked out the window, and felt a sinking sensation in the pit of his stomach. The place was enormous. With the late afternoon sunlight gilding its stone façade to a rich old gold tone, and the long line of trees with new spring leaves just showing, it was more than imposing – it was the absolute symbol of old wealth and power, and all of the things about the *ton* that challenged him, every day.

"Tell me again why I agreed to let you drop me into this pit of society vipers?"

Setford laughed, loud and long. Then smiled at him.

"Because you need the practice. And, more importantly, they need to see you. And see that the Branley girls accept you, and welcome you as the new holder of the Tillingford title. The slightest sign of resentment on their part would give the old biddies all they need to cut you completely. Conversely, their acceptance will be the first step to everyone accepting you. Stop worrying. You are more than capable of coping. And the girls, and Rotherhithe, like you. Take a deep breath, and just do it, as if you've been travelling in this rank of society all your life."

"Easy for you to say! Right now, I feel that facing a battalion of the French army would be more manageable."

Setford laughed again, but there was nothing nasty to it. It was the laughter of companionship and understanding, and Gerald appreciated the lightening of the moment.

The carriage reached the portico and stopped. A footman rushed out to open the door and let down the steps. Gerald, surprised that his legs held him, descended after Setford and followed him up the grand stairs to the door. A butler greeted them, and ushered them to a salon, announcing them at the door.

He had not thought it possible for his stomach to sink further – but it did. The large room was filled with a positive horde of men and women of the *ton*, all eating, drinking, and gossiping. A man moved towards them, and he recognised their host, the Duke of Rotherhithe, with some relief. As he greeted Rotherhithe, the two Branley girls appeared beside him, their faces wreathed in genuine smiles of welcome. He began to feel just a little better about things.

Setford, greeting Rotherhithe, who was an old friend, warmly, made a small noise of satisfaction at the girls' approach.

"Baron Tillingford, wonderful to see you again!" Georgiana, the younger girl, spoke first, pleasure and real enthusiasm in her voice.

"And you, Lady Georgiana, Lady Cordelia." He bowed over their hands in turn, making, he thought, a creditable job of looking natural about it. He was beyond grateful for the greeting, for, as they had been announced, a hush had fallen across the room, and all eyes had turned in their direction.

With the conversation stilled, he could see that those present were mostly of high station, and included a collection of the lamentable 'cream of the crop' of the eligible young men of the *ton,* and their fathers. The ladies appeared to be the mothers and sisters of those young men, and their eyes upon him assessed, deciding whether he was to be disdained, or to be hunted as a possible husband. He barely prevented himself from shuddering.

One man seemed out of place – he held himself with the natural bearing of the aristocracy, yet his clothes were older, somewhat out of fashion, visibly worn, and he stood to one side, obviously excluded from the general run of conversation. Gerald felt an immediate affinity with the man – one of them, and yet not. His curiosity was aroused.

Rotherhithe swept them along, towing them around the room, performing introductions, until Gerald's head spun trying to keep track of it all. Last to be introduced, almost as if Rotherhithe was uncomfortable with his presence, was the man who seemed out of place.

"Gerald Otford, Baron Tillingford, may I make known, Oliver Kentworthy, the Marquess of Dartworth?"

They bowed to each other, eyes meeting, both wary, yet interested. Introductions done, Rotherhithe swept Setford away to chat about old times, leaving Gerald to cope on his own. The girls had been swept up by some chattering group of females, although Lady Georgiana had not looked pleased.

Turning back to Dartworth, Gerald searched desperately for a conversational opening. The other man, a quirk of a half-smile on his lips, rescued him.

"Do I sense that you have as little liking for this sort of gathering as I do?" The forthright comment was startling, but welcome.

"Indeed, to my chagrin, I must admit that to be the case, if you are anywhere as uninspired by this chattering collection of well-bred gossips as you look to be."

The other man's half-smile became a genuine grin.

"And that would be almost the first honest answer I've had from anyone in weeks!"

Suddenly, inexplicably, comfortable, they settled to talk. A fact which drew the attention of most of the room, after a while, and not necessarily in a positive way, from the expressions on faces. Gerald wondered what Dartworth had done, to earn the obvious censure he faced.

By the time that dinner was called, he knew. They had, in each other, found someone they could talk to, and Dartworth had shared the truth of his situation – a situation that horrified Gerald. He respected the man for his courage, and his willingness to get past his noble heritage and work to survive. No-one who had been in France and Spain, in the field, would judge a man for worn clothes or calloused hands. The way that the *ton* treated Dartworth made him even more uncomfortable with his own newly ennobled status.

For a while, Lady Georgiana came to join their conversation, looking back to Rotherhithe and her sister with an expression almost rebellious, and he wondered what was behind *that*. She was, as she had been the previous time he had met her, a delight.

Her keen intelligence positively shone in her conversation, and he could see that Dartworth was very taken with her, and that, it seemed, she was rather taken with him too. As a Marquess, he was certainly of suitable rank to be a potential husband for her, but, he suspected, that rebellious look might have something to do with his lack of funds and his other history making him ineligible in Rotherhithe's eyes.

Gerald's curiosity pulled at him – he wanted to know what was going on here. But he certainly couldn't ask! Perhaps conversation over dinner would reveal more. He offered Lady Georgiana his arm, and she took it gracefully, allowing him to lead her into dinner.

~~~~~

The dinner conversation proved to be ordinary, as if everyone, after yesterday's vigorous discussion, was on their best behaviour. Georgiana sighed – how boring. Still, it meant that she could eat, and surreptitiously watch Oliver, hoping for some moments when their eyes might meet. She was so grateful for the fact that Otford had chosen to talk with Oliver. Even more now, she considered Otford a most welcome friend.

Once dinner was done, they once again retired to the library, for games, and conversation. In the library, the servants had provided fresh carafes of sherry and madeira for the guests and, as they entered the spacious room, Rotherhithe invited Oliver to the chess board. The Duke smiled and assured the young Marquess that they were only playing for sport and not for money. It was obvious to Setford, Georgiana and Gerald that Oliver did not find any amusement in the comment.
~~~~~

But he was a guest in the Duke's house and, in spite of his slightly worn and inelegant clothing, he was determined to conduct himself with all the decorum he could muster. Georgiana took a seat nearby and declined the offer of a glass of sherry. She had never been fond of drinking and preferred to concentrate on the game being played before her.

There were several moments during the game when it was obvious to her that either Oliver was uncommonly inept at chess or that he was deliberately avoiding the chance of winning. The Duke slammed the beautiful table with his hand and called out "Checkmate!" The entire room could hear him announce his victory. Oliver bowed his head and saluted the victor. The Duke was beaming. Georgiana stood and approached the inlaid mahogany chess table.

"I would happily play you, if Your Grace would be willing."

The Duke looked up at her and the smile stayed upon his lips but disappeared completely from his eyes. He might genuinely like the young woman, but he did not like the potential of being beaten at chess by her, before his guests.

"In fact, Your Grace, I would be more than willing to play for a prize. If you would wager?"

The Duke sat frozen in his seat, never taking his eyes from the young Lady before him. Finally, he spoke.

"Nothing would give me more pleasure, my girl, but I believe I am expected at the card table." He rose from his seat and indicated Oliver. "Let us see if the Marquess here can provide you with some entertainment at the chess board. Dartworth? Are you ready to play again? If I have not completely exhausted you with my victory?"

Oliver stood to welcome Georgiana to the table.

"I will take the Duke's seat", she said softly, slipping into the chair, and beginning to set up the pieces for the new game, "to my eye, it would seem that he was uncommonly lucky to have defeated you."

For a moment, she was sure that he blushed, but he recovered quickly enough.

"It was only good manners to permit my host to savour the fruits of victory."

"Ah," replied Georgiana. "It seems I must have mislaid my manners, for I trounced him most soundly at the board the evening we arrived."

There was a twinkle in her eye and Oliver smiled again.

"No wonder he would not play you again. And, should you have wagered, what prize would you have claimed in victory, dear Lady?"

"Five thousand pounds. That I might give it to you."

Oliver's jaw opened and closed twice without him making a sound. "Georgiana. That is not a subject for jesting."

"And I am not jesting." She looked into his blue eyes and saw that he was deeply moved by her words. "I believe that you may now make the first move."

The two were unaware that Setford and Gerald had settled in two chairs nearby – close enough to overhear the conversation. Nothing was said, but Setford met Gerald's eyes and raised an eyebrow in interest. Gerald simply mouthed *'later'* to him and nodded.

This time, Oliver did not feel he had to pander to his opponent's sensitivities. Although he was initially thrown off by his emotional reaction to what she had said about the five thousand pounds, he soon settled and became absorbed in the game. He played seriously and well. Georgiana was quietly impressed at his grasp of the game, at his patience and his ability to think through the possibilities.

After twenty minutes, the spell was broken by the Duke's laughter as he won yet another hand of cards.

"They let him win to maintain his favour," Oliver whispered across the table.

"I guessed as much. Almost everyone lets him win as a courtesy but he must know that they play him too, letting him gather up his winnings and boast of his empty victories. After what he did for my sister, unmasking Lord Edward's cheating, I know that he is far better at cards than he seems, and far better at cards than he is at chess! He will see, immediately, what they do. So why does he allow it to continue?"

"If they think he is less astute than he is, he has an advantage over them. Rich men rule the world, Georgiana. Everyone must dance to their tunes."

"Not I, Oliver. I want to dance to my own tune. Except that I can't actually dance!"

He laughed and leaned a little closer across the pieces.

"Perhaps you would permit me to teach you a few steps?" he looked into her eyes. "But only as long as it gave you pleasure."

Now it was Georgiana's turn to smile. She found the suggestion quite appealing, despite the fact that she'd never been interested in dancing since the day she was born. Perhaps, it would be something entirely different and unexpected with the dashing Oliver Kentworthy.

Eventually, the young Marquess sat back and announced a draw.

"We're going around in circles here and it's becoming obvious that we could play for many hours without a conclusion. It is quite evident that you are a most worthy opponent. Possibly," he smiled at her with his even white teeth, "also the most attractive opponent in the room!"

She laughed.

"Only in this room? Have I such little competition?"

"Well, perhaps the most attractive player in all of Christendom."

"Better. That offers a wider compass for comparison."

At the card table, the Duke gathered up his winnings, wagging his finger at his guests with a broad grin.

"Now you'll be telling everyone that my table may well be the costliest in the county, on account of your losses at the gaming table!"

He laughed good naturedly at the expressions on a few of the young men – it seemed that the losses of some were genuine, not intended, and not so lightly felt. Setford was quietly amused, knowing just how good at cards Philip actually was.

Smiling, Rotherhithe continued.

"Gentlemen, let us adjourn to the smoking room and enjoy a pipe or two of Virginia's finest tobacco. Ladies, you will find tea, and a further supply of sherry and madeira, in the main salon. If you hear singing, fear not for we shall only sing of your beauty and raise toasts to your health!"

Oliver bowed to her, and departed with the other gentlemen. Georgiana took a comfortable seat in the great salon, yet she did not feel entirely at her ease in the company of so many aristocratic ladies. Never having had a London Season, given her youth, for she had turned seventeen only a month ago, and the timing of her father's death, she had not had much chance to be about in society, even had she been remotely interested in doing so.

She instantly became aware, yet again, of their cool appraisal, their critical glances, the way that they assessed her dress, her manners and her speech. Every time she was in the presence of these people, it was the same. Once again, she felt like a prize exhibit at a cattle auction. A cattle auction – not even a thoroughbred bloodstock sale! The conversation appeared seemly and polite on the surface, but it soon degenerated into the kind of gossiping that Georgiana detested with every fibre of her being.

She remembered only too well how much of a bore she found these dreadful social occasions. Now she was stuck in the middle of such an unavoidable event. She fervently wished that she, like Miss Millpost, could simply settle in a chair in a quiet corner, with a glass of madeira, and ignore it all.

But she could not even stop up her ears and was obliged to hear every word that was being spoken by two older ladies, who were seated near to her on a silk-cushioned sofa.

"A rogue, you say, my dear? That would be the least of it."

"Do you know more of him than I, my dear?"

"I heard directly from Lady Charlotte herself that's he's a rake. He's a scoundrel. That he consorts with milkmaids and serving wenches. He's an unmannered ape. No wonder his father lost everything at the gaming tables."

"Well, my dear, the apple never falls far from the tree. Bad blood, the Kentworthys. Bad seed the whole lot of them. Nothing good will ever come of him, of that I am quite sure."

Georgiana suddenly realised that they were speaking of Oliver. She tried not to show her alarm at what was being said yet her curiosity ran away with her like a team of wild horses.

"Can't keep his hands off the tavern girls and we all know what they are like, my dear, do we not? The lowest of the low."

"The father was the same. Young Dartworth has inherited all of his father's vices and not one penny of the family fortune!"

They both laughed, a braying laugh like a pair of mules, and Georgiana didn't know if she wanted to bang their silly heads together for speaking so rudely about Oliver, or for not telling the truth. But... what if it was the truth? She felt confused by what she had heard. Inside, she felt hurt and bruised. Serving girls? Tavern wenches? Hayseed milkmaids? It was too much to bear. Was he so smooth and charming with every slatternly dockside doxy? Had she been taken in, like a fool?

She could not bear to think about it. She had been so certain that he was a good man, just in a difficult situation. But… what if she was wrong? Suddenly close to tears, as much from confusion and frustration as from hurt, she considered just leaving the room.

She stood and made her way to a corner of the room near the doors, to stand alone not far from the chair in which Miss Millpost now dozed, blessedly free from any need to socialise with the ladies who filled the room. At least here she could avoid the stares of the other ladies. A conversation caught her attention when her name was spoken.

She heard nothing really new. The women only confirmed that every eager hound in the aristocratic pack was bent on claiming her dowry, and the rich income from her lands, as the valuable prize of matrimony. They were baying for her inheritance. Not for her.

And she had thought that Oliver was different from the others. Now it seemed that, perhaps, the only difference between him and them was that he was poor whilst they were rich.

And all that meant was that he needed her dowry more than most. For, surely, there was some grain of truth in the gossip — things might be exaggerated, but were rarely invented from whole cloth! How could she have been so cruelly deceived?

All heads turned, and every conversation came to an abrupt halt as a commotion broke out in the corridor beyond the salon doors. There were shouts, thumps and raised voices, then the sound of someone crying out, apparently in pain.

Unthinking of her own safety, or anything else, overcome by her insatiable curiosity, Georgiana threw open the salon doors and stepped into the candlelit corridor.

To her astonishment, she saw Oliver, being told to stand against a wall by the Duke. Two young men were lying on the floor at his feet with blood on their faces, and it was clear that Oliver must have knocked them down. Indeed, a visible smear of blood upon his fist confirmed that fact. Georgiana heard a Lady behind her gasp in horror and mutter.

"The brute! He deserves a whipping!"

The Duke was merely looking at Oliver rather than attempting to lay his hands upon the powerfully built young man. Oliver seemed strangely calm, despite the fact that he had just struck the two gentlemen. Georgiana could only wonder at his reason. The Duke stepped back and pointed towards the entrance hall.

"Leave my house immediately, Dartworth, or I shall summon the footmen to deal with you."

Oliver nodded and, in that moment, he caught a fleeting glimpse of Georgiana standing in the salon doorway. He smiled briefly, sadly, before turning on his heel and marching purposefully towards the great house's magnificent entrance.

The Duke urged the other men to pick up the two stricken nobles and then ushered them all back into the smoking room amidst a great deal of muttering, and more than a few words of coarse and ungentlemanly language. Then he turned his attention towards the ladies. He tried to affect a calm manner, and offered his widest smile to them.

"My apologies to each and all of you for that unfortunate incident. The young Marquess has a hot head and, although I did not witness the event, I am told that he was the one who started the altercation. Once again, please accept my apologies for the unfortunate disturbance to an otherwise perfectly enjoyable evening."

The ladies bobbed and curtsied in acknowledgement of the Duke's attempts to calm them and returned like a flock of obedient sheep to the comfort and warmth of the salon. Except for Georgiana. She was staring at the blood on the polished marble floor and fearing the worst. Perhaps it really was true. And Oliver Kentworthy was nothing more than a scoundrel, a rogue, a hot-headed fool and a rake. The Duke noticed her standing alone in the doorway to the salon. He approached her and ventured to put a fatherly hand on her shoulder.

"I am truly sorry, my girl. I know that you have conceived some fondness for the rascal. I would have preferred that you did not have to witness his brutality at first hand."

"I am deeply shocked by what I have now heard and seen of this man, your Grace."

She looked into his eyes and she could see the care that he felt for her.

"I know. I know, Georgiana. He was never going to be a suitable match for you. You deserve much better than Kentworthy. I regret ever inviting him here."

Slowly, with tears in her eyes, Georgiana nodded her head in agreement.

"You must choose very soon, my girl. Time is running short. Make your choice from the fine young gentlemen who have come to pay court to you. Choose soon, my girl, or I shall be obliged to keep my word to your late father and carry out his wishes by choosing a husband for you."

At that moment, Cordelia walked up to her sister and placed a comforting arm around her waist.

"Choose soon, my darling sister, or Philip will, indeed, have to choose for you. You know that we only want the best for you."

Georgiana nodded but, in her heart, she felt that her world was dissolving around her, spinning madly out of control. She was not even sure if she would survive this terrible ordeal.

For that matter, she was not sure that she wanted to survive it. Everything that she had thought she knew of the people surrounding her now seemed cast into doubt. Was she really such a bad judge of character? Had she been so terribly wrong about Oliver?

<div align="center">~~~~~</div>

Oliver was saddened by the whole turn of affairs, but unsurprised. No-one here was likely to take his word on anything.

He was the inconvenient one who disturbed their sense of the rightness of their world. Well, he still had his dignity. For now, a room at the local inn would suffice – at least until his limited funds ran out.

But the look in Lady Georgiana's eyes, as she had watched him from the salon doorway, would haunt him. His heart ached that he had caused her such pain – and even more that she should, it seemed, so easily believe him the uncouth brute he had been presented as. He had felt, just for a little there, that, perhaps, just perhaps, she was different, and might be able to see the man beyond the clothes and the gossip. It would seem not.

~~~~~

Setford and Gerald, arriving in the door to the hall, just as Rotherhithe ordered Dartworth from the house, allowed the other men to convey the fallen past them, and listened to Rotherhithe's words to the Ladies. Something was not right here. Gerald could not believe it of Oliver. This was not the actions he would expect from the man he had conversed with this afternoon. He turned to Setford.

"Why would he...?"

"I don't know. But I am quite certain we don't have the full story. Still, Rotherhithe seems convinced that its clear cut, and it's his house."

Troubled, they turned back to follow the other men – perhaps hearing the story from the two injured men would clarify things a bit. But that was not to be.

The two moaned and performed about their injuries in a manner worthy of the stage. Gerald was quite certain that neither of them would have lasted more than a few days at war.
~~~~~

Their dramatic declarations of being set upon for no reason, and beaten to the floor seemed ridiculous to him, yet everyone else, except Setford, seemed ready to take them at their word, instantly.

The brandy Setford handed him was most welcome, although he was strongly tempted to dash it in the moaning gentleman's face, to bring him to his senses. Reminding himself that he was now a polite gentleman, and simply could not do such a thing, Gerald settled in a chair in a quiet corner, to continue watching the drama unfold.

Setford simply listened, every sense alert, his clever mind integrating all of what he had seen and heard, looking for a logical answer. He wished, at that moment, that Hunter was here. Of all the Hounds, Hunter was the one with the most astute mind, the one who could take a mass of disparate information, and find the truth amongst it, almost magically. If he could convince him, one day, in the hopefully distant future, Hunter might be the man he handed the spymaster's role to, when he himself retired. Not that Hunter had the faintest inkling of that yet.

Chapter Seven

Georgiana slept fitfully that night, woken by strange dreams and haunted by the vision of Oliver Kentworthy leaving the Duke's great house in disgrace. A cad. A bounder. A scoundrel. A rogue. The words of the other ladies echoed in her mind and drove splinters of ice into her heart. She woke in the early hours and found her pillow damp with tears.

In the distance, a fox barked in the darkness and the household dogs answered the plaintive cry, with a melancholy howling that seemed to come more from the depths of Georgiana's tortured soul.

She was tormented and distraught, feeling hopeless and, in many ways, abandoned. She could not explain why but she felt Oliver's departure most deeply and she wondered why the young Marquess seemed so important to her.

In so many ways, the Duke and her sister were right: Oliver was a terrible choice as a husband.

He was as poor as a church mouse, he had a most unfortunate reputation, he had spent time as a common labourer in the former Colonies, he was reputed to consort with tavern girls and serving wenches and his politics were only just short of revolutionary. He was impossible.

And now it seemed that he had a violent temper.

She rolled over and pulled the soft blanket up beneath her chin. The dying embers in the fireplace cast a dull, red glow across the rugs as Georgiana closed her eyes once more and resolved to sleep. Sleep, however, seemed utterly out of reach. Her thoughts went round and round, considering her impossible situation, and finding no answers to her problems.

The Duke's wedding was approaching and she would have to make a decision about her choice of husband, or her sister's bridegroom would make the choice for her. She needed to rest. She desperately needed more time. But time was running out and the moment of decision would soon overtake her.

A few hours later, as the cheerful chambermaid attended to Georgiana's fireplace and brought her a basin of hot water, Cordelia knocked gently upon the door and stepped into her sister's bedchamber to bid her good morning. Georgiana looked exhausted.

"My poor sister. You look as if you haven't slept a wink all night. You're going to need more than a touch of rouge this morning, my dear!" Cordelia sat down on the comfortable bed and held her sister's hand. "Georgiana, I pray you don't feel that we are trying to rush you into something that you do not want."

She could see that Georgiana had been crying. She held Georgiana's hand more tightly.

"Philip would much prefer that you make your own choice. He was very worried that you might make a terrible error and choose Oliver Kentworthy. But if you cannot choose, and Philip understands how difficult it must be for you, he will act on Papa's behalf and make the match for you. He's very fond of you, you know? He only wants what's best for you."

Georgiana felt the hot tears in her eyes again. She could not tell if she was weeping because of her sister's love for her or because she had lost Oliver – the only one of the possible suitors here who had seemed to actually see her as a person. Whatever the cause, she felt thoroughly wretched.

"Come! It's breakfast time. Rouse yourself from your bed. Wash and get dressed and don't spare the rouge. I'll send one of the maids to you with a potion of belladonna for your eyes. We can't have you looking like you slept in a ditch! And remember to smile. This is supposed to be a time for celebration!"

With a light kiss on her sister's tear-stained cheek, Cordelia rose from the bed and hurried away to find the eye-brightening potion that would disguise her sister's lack of sleep. Ladies had to be cunning sometimes, and employ the wiles of nature to enhance their appearance.

Today was just such a day.

~~~~~

The day went by in a blur, and Georgiana hated the way that all she heard was scandalised gossip about the events of the previous evening.
~~~~~

As soon as she could, she convinced Miss Millpost that a walk would be a wonderful idea, and set off, determinedly, at a pace which Miss Millpost found hard to match. She only realised that fact when Miss Millpost, sounding rather breathless, called out to her.

"Lady Georgiana! Do you think that you might, perhaps, be able to manage a more ladylike pace?"

The words were laced with both frustration and sarcasm, mixed with amusement, and Georgiana stopped, instantly contrite. She genuinely liked Miss Millpost, most of the time, and had certainly not intended to run her to exhaustion trying to keep up.

Once Miss Millpost reached her, they continued, side by side, at a much gentler pace.

"And where might we be going, my Lady? For it seems to me that you have a definite destination in mind."

"I am almost certain that you can guess, Miss Millpost. Where have I always gone when I'm feeling out of sorts?"

"Ah. The stables, then? And does this establishment boast kittens or puppies in the stables? For that is usually your entertainment of choice when you are feeling blue-devilled."

Georgiana laughed, beginning to feel better already.

"I have no idea – but I plan to find out. And, if there are kittens or puppies, to be horribly unladylike and let them crawl all over me with their dirty little paws."

Miss Millpost sighed and shook her head. But she was smiling. This was her Georgiana – not the moody girl of the last two weeks.

Upon reaching the stables, Georgiana discovered, to her delight, that there were, indeed, both kittens and puppies. She fell to her knees in the straw, and did as she had said – gathered them into her lap and played with them. For just a little while, she pushed aside her misery and all thought of marriage, suitors, the *ton*, and her heart-breaking uncertainty about Oliver's character.

~~~~~

Gerald was oddly relieved, and a little ashamed of that fact, to realise, the next morning, that the scandalous scuffle involving the Marquess of Dartworth was still the uppermost thing on the minds of the crowd of house guests at Canterwood Park. For, as a result, they were, on the whole, ignoring Gerald completely – which he found far more comfortable than being the centre of their potentially censorious attention.

He broke his fast sparingly, comfortable in Setford's company and, with barely a word spoken between them, they left the house early, to enjoy a ride through the extensive grounds of the Park, taking advantage of Rotherhithe's generous offer of the use of his horses. Just stepping out of the room full of gossip was wonderful. The oh, so respectable, members of the *ton* resembled a flock of vultures gathered to wait for the final moments of an injured creature. All they could speak of was how Dartworth should be punished for his actions.

Yet, to Gerald, it still seemed wrong – he was certain that there was more to the story. He had, during the war, interrogated far too many men – he had a deeply developed sense of when a man was not telling everything that there was to tell.
~~~~~

Twenty minutes later, mounted on a mare of extraordinary quality, he raced beside Setford across the rolling hills of the estate. The wind in his hair blew away his sense of frustration, and he allowed himself to relax, to simply enjoy. Eventually they pulled the blowing horses back to a walk, following a shaded path along the banks of a river, companionably side by side.

"I'm still not happy with the events of yesterday. Something about the whole thing just feels wrong." Setford stared away into the distance, speaking almost as if to himself.

"Neither am I. Every instinct says that those puffed up popinjays that Dartworth flattened were not telling the whole story. They demonstrated every sign of being men who were hiding something."

Setford turned and looked at Gerald, considering the younger man's expression.

"That would be your formal assessment, as a man trained in extracting information from those who do not wish to give it?"

Gerald flinched, his intense dark blue eyes becoming shadowed with some sorrow or pain. A small shudder ran through him, causing the mare to quicken her pace in response. He eased her back, breathing deeply, and waited a moment before responding.

"Yes, if you put it that way. It is a skill I wish I had never learnt. But, once learnt, such things cannot be unlearnt. And the application of such knowledge has left me with memories that will haunt me forever. But, in this case, I supposed such a sense of things is useful."

"I hope so."

"I may, perchance, be biased in this assessment. I liked Dartworth when I spent that time talking with him. I found him refreshingly forthright and honest, a man not afraid to have an opinion, but not rash. He would not have survived the circumstances he has been through if he had truly been a hot-headed fool. So – biased or not, I find the claims of his 'victims' not entirely convincing. I do not see Dartworth as a man who would attack someone for no reason."

"Indeed, I would agree with that evaluation."

"It was, almost, as if those two who felt the force of his displeasure were actively avoiding answering any questions. Their performance would have done well on a stage, it was so drama filled. And those who provide a dramatic performance usually do so to distract from some much more important fact or activity. Much though it disturbs me to say this, much though it makes me revolted by my own capabilities, part of me would like nothing better than to put them to a true interrogation, to extract the truth from them by whatever means it took. What kind of person does that make me?"

"A loyal one. A man who values his country, his companions and the truth more than the social graces. A man who was brave enough to carry out the necessary, yet unsavoury, tasks that war demands, but which few are capable of doing. Do not despise yourself, Otford – you are a stronger and better man than you realise."

Gerald's mouth twisted into a cynical half smile, but he said nothing more for some time, as they rode on along the path, the small river gurgling over the rocks beside them, and the morning sun burning the last of the mist from its surface.

"Setford, you are an old friend to Rotherhithe, might you be able to convince him to question those young fops further?"

"Perhaps, perhaps. Although, Philip has always been a man who can become rather over fond of his own ideas. It can take some effort to shift him from an opinion, no matter how reasonable a person he is most of the time. Still, you are right to ask. I'll speak to him and see what comes of it. I won't feel comfortable until I know the truth of what happened in that hallway, before we all heard the scuffling. Young Dartworth may be rather controversial in his political and societal views, but I've no indication, from any of my sources, that he is, in any way, actually revolutionary. Rather the opposite, actually."

Gerald nodded, happy to let the discussion drop at that point, and to go back to considering far more pleasant things, such as the horse beneath him and the delightful scenery around him. By the time they reached the stables on their return, he was at peace with himself again, for now, pondering Setford's words about the sort of man he was. Setford, it seemed, saw a rather different man than he saw himself as.

In the stables, they discovered Lady Georgiana, amidst a tangle of puppies, her skirt covered in straw and dust, but looking happier than she had seemed since their arrival. They dismounted, passing the horses to the grooms, and joined Miss Millpost in observing Lady Georgiana. Miss Millpost curtseyed, smiling at their approach.

"Some habits cannot easily be educated out of young Ladies." Her smile belied the mock severity of her tone.

"And why would one want to? Surely the ability to play unreservedly is one to be treasured."

Gerald spoke with obvious sincerity, smiling as he watched the puppies make a concerted attack upon Lady Georgiana. She allowed them to tumble her flat to the straw, laughing as they licked at her face.

Setford allowed a few moments to pass, before bowing to both women.

"Ladies, I am afraid we must leave you to your entertainment, for we have business to attend to in the house. Do enjoy your day."

Drawing Gerald with him, he walked out into the spring sunshine and returned to the house, intent upon seeking Rotherhithe out at the earliest opportunity.

∿∿∿∿∿

They found Rotherhithe in his Study, just finishing a discussion with his estate manager. Philip looked up when they tapped on the door, and smiled with real pleasure.

"Setford, Otford, do come in and take a seat. What can I do for you?"

"Rotherhithe, old man, we've just been for a ride about your excellent estate. I have to thank you for the use of your bloodstock. Quality indeed. But, while we were out, we've been discussing the events of yesterday. Yes, yes, I know that everyone has, but I hope that we are rather more considered in our thinking than that flock of gossipy scandal mongers you've invited to eat and drink you dry."

The Duke laughed – Setford went right to the heart of things, as usual.

"And the result of your conversation brings you here, now?"

"Yes, it does. It is my... professional... opinion, that there is more to the story than we've been told. Something about the events of last night does not ring true. I'd like your permission to question the two 'victims' of the event further. You're aware of my role – it's my business to be certain of the truth behind what goes on in society, for the security of the country, and the Prince Regent. But it's your house – and your decision."

Rotherhithe looked startled at the formality of this pronouncement, and eyed Gerald with interest, wondering what his role was, that Setford had included him here. He leant back in his chair and thought.

"I really can't see why you'd think that there was anything more to it. It seems remarkably obvious to me. Young Dartworth has spent too long amongst the lower classes, dealing with things by brute force, and has forgotten how to be a gentleman. I'll admit that the other young men who are guests here have not treated him well, have not shown themselves in the best light either, but they have not resorted to violence. It seems very clear that Dartworth's resentment of their attitudes, and their wealth, finally overflowed into action of the most reprehensible kind."

The Duke shook his head sadly, and gave a little shrug, as if pushing the whole thing aside.

"Surely, Rotherhithe, it cannot be that simple? The boy has been under very strained circumstances, but I've never heard of him resorting to violence. His father may have been an inveterate gambler and womaniser, but he was never a violent or intentionally dishonourable man."

"Ah, but his father never spent time working in the fields alongside a collection of revolutionary commoners, did he? Who knows what habits young Oliver developed during his years in the Americas? Are you suggesting that I doubt the word of Bentwick and Eggmorton? They are from impeccable bloodlines, families without the least breath of scandal touching them – why would I doubt them? No, I most certainly cannot allow you to question them, as if they were common criminals. You will have to be content with my decision, I'm afraid."

Gerald forced himself not to grind his teeth in frustration at the Duke's words. The man was, although generally a reasonable person, from all that he had seen, obviously exactly as Setford had said – very hard to shift from his position once he had formed an opinion on a matter. Every part of Gerald's war trained instincts screamed at him that those two 'victims' were lying – or at least not telling the whole truth. But how could he discover the truth, if Rotherhithe wouldn't even allow them to talk to the men about it?

"You're quite certain, Rotherhithe? I can't convince you otherwise?"

Setford's voice was as calm as ever, but Gerald could see the tiny signs of tension in him, the strength with which his hand grasped the arm of the chair, the tiny narrowing of his piercing grey eyes. It took long exposure to the man to become aware of such things – he wondered why Rotherhithe ignored it, for surely, as an old friend of Setford's, he should notice it as much as Gerald did?

"If there's nothing else I can do for you?" Rotherhithe looked at them enquiringly – clearly, the conversation was at an end.

Setford sighed.

"If that is your final word on it, then no, nothing else. I hope, Rotherhithe, that you don't come to regret this decision."

They rose, bowed, and left the room, both wondering how on earth they could investigate when the Duke had expressly demanded that they not do so.

Chapter Eight

The following morning, the two sisters were seated next to each other, with a basket of freshly baked bread and fine cups of hot coffee, as the servants brought the breakfast dishes to the table. The other guests had not emerged from their chambers and the young women had the elegant dining table to themselves for a change.

Not even Miss Millpost had joined them yet. Georgiana, perhaps a little uncharitably, suspected that an over indulgence in madeira may have something to do with that too.

Cordelia smiled.

"Too much wine and cognac last night, I'll wager. The guests seem to enjoy making free with Philip's hospitality. There'll be many a sore head this morning, I expect!"

Georgiana nodded. "It will serve them right for their lack of sobriety. Yet I have not seen the Duke in his cups once since we arrived. He seems to prefer moderation over excess, and that is a most commendable virtue, dear sister."

"He has many virtues, to be sure. He told me that the king's own physician advised him to drink less, or else risk the gout as he gets older, and he has most wisely heeded the advice. So, he is a wise and virtuous lord! And who could not possibly love him?"

"You are most fortunate in Papa's choice of husband for you, dear sister, and in the fact that you are in love with him. Of that there is no doubt."

"I know. I am truly blessed and I have noted that often Philip prefers to take his ease with a good twist of tobacco amongst his beloved falcons. He finds more peace amongst the society of birds than amongst the finely plumed gentlemen of the county."

"But quiet now, dear sister, for your Lord approaches."

The Duke strode into the dining room and each of the servants paused to turn towards him and bow. It was a rigidly upheld formality that reminded everyone of their position in the household and of their duty and loyalty to the noble head of the house. Woe betide any servant who neglected to bow their heads in the presence of the Duke – or at least, not whilst the house was full of gossiping nobility!

A noble's title and power were never to be taken lightly., as far as most of the *ton* were concerned, and Philip had no interest in giving them any fodder for more gossip!

Cordelia and Georgiana both rose at the Duke's approach and curtsied most prettily to acknowledge his presence. He smiled broadly and lightly waved them back to their seats as he took his place at the head of the table. Servants bustled around him, bringing him fresh bread and coffee, and offering other dishes for his choice. He leaned a little closer to Georgiana.

"Did you sleep well, my girl?"

"Your Grace, I fear not."

The Duke looked a little startled at the frank admission. Cordelia shrugged with a small shift of her shoulders as if that would explain all that was to be said of her headstrong sister.

"Well, never mind. Georgiana, my girl, time is pressing and it is clear to me that you are completely unable to make a decision for yourself and choose the fortunate fellow who is to be your husband."

The air suddenly seemed to thicken and Georgiana felt the atmosphere closing in around her chest and throat.

"Therefore, in accordance with your late father's wishes, I have chosen to decide the issue on your behalf. It is not something that I have undertaken lightly. I am considering my decision, and will inform you, late this afternoon, of the conclusion I have reached."

Georgiana gasped, finding herself at a complete loss for words.

With that statement, the Duke broke open a steaming hot roll, added a curl of butter and a spoonful of damson jam and broke his fast with a satisfied nod, as a servant poured his first cup of coffee of the day. He fully intended to enjoy his breakfast.

Cordelia and Georgiana finished their meal and asked the Duke for his permission to withdraw from the dining table. The Duke nodded his assent, understanding that the sisters would probably need to talk. They repaired to the great salon to sit in front of the great fire that warmed the room and lent a welcome glow to their cheeks.

The salon was, thankfully empty of any aristocratic guests – Georgiana was certain that she would have no option but to flee to her room, should any of them appear. Her head was spinning – in but a few hours from now, she would know her fate, would know which of the unbearable young men she would be forced to wed. Cordelia gently touched her sister's hand and spoke quietly.

"I know you cannot be anything but surprised by this new development, my dear, but you must trust Philip completely in these matters. He knows that you are headstrong and wilful, but he really is very fond of you and only wants what is best."

Georgiana nodded, still confused and reeling from the sudden revelation that she was to be married, to a man not of her choosing, a man that she would barely know. It was all so sudden. Her head was spinning.

"It won't be so bad. You will be marrying a titled man. Whoever Philip chooses for you, you can be certain of having a title and influence as a result of your marriage."

Georgiana nodded again, tears spilling from her eyes and coursing down her cheeks.

"Come, my little sister. Do not weep. Dry your pretty eyes for this is surely a time for joy. We shall soon both be married and you will have Papa's estate once more and live in a magnificent house with all the wealth and servants your heart could desire."

It was too much and Georgiana covered her face with her hands as the tears flowed more copiously than ever. Cordelia drew a lace kerchief from her sleeve and dried the tears from her sister's cheeks.

"Now, now, little one. Enough of these tears. You are beginning to appear ungrateful for the good fortune that is being bestowed upon you, and that will never do."

"Have I no other choice, Cordelia?"

"No, my sweet. You do not. And there are not many Ladies who would turn up their noses at the chance to marry a wealthy titled man."

Georgiana sighed deeply and with a small shudder took her sister's kerchief and removed the last droplets of moisture from the corner of her eyes.

"Very well, Cordelia. Let us have done with this sadness. If I am to be married, then the least I can do is to show my gratitude to the Duke for his kindliness on my behalf. For I know that he intends it as kindliness, and that he is being true to Papa's wishes, even if I am not happy with this at all."

Cordelia beamed at her sister, pleased that she was finally seeing sense. She began to believe that everything would work out well in the end. Finally, she felt free to concentrate on her own wedding.

~~~~~

When the Duke summoned Georgiana to his study, as the late afternoon light faded into dusk, she was prepared. Not happy, certainly not happy, but prepared to present herself with dignity, and do as her father had wished. Inside, a small still voice was crying, wishing that things had been different, imagining a world in which she might marry a man such as Oliver, who saw her, really saw her, not just her wealth.
~~~~~

She pushed those thoughts and feelings aside. Might-have-beens would make no different to reality.

She tapped on the Study door and entered at the Duke's invitation. He was standing by the fireplace, a serious expression on his face. He looked, she thought, almost nervous. Which was ridiculous – what did he have to be nervous about? Perhaps he feared that she would rebel, would do something outrageous? Let him worry. She would behave with as much dignity as she could manage.

Georgiana did not speak, she simply bobbed a curtsey and waited. The Duke cleared his throat, and came to stand before her.

"My dear Lady Georgiana, I know that you had hoped to make your own choice, to be as lucky as your sister, and to find yourself in love with the man that you would marry, yet you have completely failed to develop even a friendship with an eligible gentleman, let alone conceive a *tendre* for one!"

Georgiana simply looked at him, still waiting.

Given that, I find myself forced to choose for you, in fulfilling your father's last wishes. I have, over the last few weeks, considered the question from all possible angles, and have concluded that the only truly suitable choice is the Earl of Bentwick. He is of suitably good family, titled, wealthy, in good health, not known to gamble excessively or drink to extremes. In short, he has all of the qualities required to provide you with the sort of life that you deserve. There it is. You have my decision."

Georgiana looked at the Duke with eyes that did not see and ears that simply could not register what he had just uttered.

The earl of Bentwick? She could not even bring the man to mind – she had, she realised, not the slightest memory of which of the annoying collection of suitors was the Earl. She drew in her breath to confirm what she had heard.

"I am to be married to the Earl of Bentwick, your Grace?"

"That is correct. Congratulations, my girl. Your engagement will be announced today at dinner. Then, tomorrow evening, we shall have a Ball in honour of your betrothal."

~~~~~

Georgiana felt numb during the lavish dinner. As the guests assembled, the Duke chose his moment perfectly to stand and raise one hand and the crowd became hushed. When he announced in his loud and clear voice that the young and splendidly attired young Earl of Bentwick was to marry the strikingly beautiful Lady Georgiana Branley, all the guests applauded politely, but it was obvious that the unsuccessful contenders for Georgiana's hand were all very disappointed at their loss. The less polite of them cast hard glances the way of the Earl, and muttered amongst themselves.

The Duke led Georgiana to the young Earl and placed her hand in his. Her heart painfully skipped a beat as she stared into the cold, aloof eyes of the young and obviously spoiled aristocrat. Georgiana curtsied and the Earl barely bent his elegantly coiffured head in acknowledgement. Georgiana was horrified. Not this vain popinjay? Not this milk-skinned boy pretending to be a man? Not this costumed mannequin with the cold, damp hand that reminded her of grasping a cold, dead fish?
~~~~~

Her heart sank even further, yet she was determined not to show anything of her deep and bitter disappointment. It would be like conceding the game before the match had even begun. She still had an ounce of pride in her heart and something stirred within her that reminded her that she would rather die than disappoint her father's memory. She smiled and noticed that the Earl could barely look at her. What was this? A groom that could not even bring himself to look at his bride?

Thankfully, she did not need to spend much time with him that evening. She was seated beside him at dinner, but, as he appeared completely uninterested in conversing with her, she simply forced a few morsels of food down her throat and said nothing. The food might as well have been dirt and dust, so hard was it to choke down. Her traitorous mind kept comparing this man, this man who would be her *husband*, with Oliver, seeing the stark difference in attitude as well as appearance. No amount of reminding herself that Oliver had proved a deception, a violent and unsuitable man, seemed to convince her heart. She wished, in that moment, that it was he at her side, not this man who might as well be a statue given how cold and unanimated he was.

As soon as she politely could, Georgiana excused herself, and went to her room. Once the maid had assisted her in preparing for bed, she crumpled into the big chair before the fire and burst into tears. If she could barely stand the duration of a dinner at his side, how would she ever manage to live with that man for the rest of her life? Even worse, how could she ever tolerate his hands upon her body – for surely, he would want an heir, and it was a wife's duty to provide her husband with one.

A little later, there was a tap at her door, and Miss Millpost entered. She was carrying a tray, and the scent of rich, slightly milky hot chocolate drifted into the room with her. She placed the tray on the side table, and disregarding her dignity, knelt by the chair and pulled Georgiana into her arms.

"Hush Miss Georgie, tears won't help. You always were brave and strong – let me see that side of you now. I know that you don't like the Duke's choice – I could see it in your face when the Earl took your hand. But you've no option. I cannot, for the life of me, work out a way around it. And I've given it a great deal of thought, let me assure you. Give him a chance – at this ball tomorrow night, surely he will woo you a little, will treat you as he should. I do so want you to be happy, my dear."

Georgiana, at these words, burst into another flood of tears, suddenly grateful for Miss Millpost's steady companionship for so much of her life. This was the woman who had taught her to use her brains, as well as her beauty – she owed it to her to try to deal with this well, rather than simply dissolving into a puddle on the floor. Taking the kerchief that Miss Millpost proffered, she dried her eyes and smiled shakily.

"That's better. Now drink this nice warm chocolate that I've brought you. There's a little posset in it to help you sleep – for you must look your best tomorrow. Even if you are not happy with the man, you must not let him see it. Start as you mean to go on. Be strong, and do not let him think that he can order you around easily. You may have to marry him, but you can at least make your own choice about how you let him treat you!"

Georgiana took the drink and sipped slowly, considering Miss Millpost's words.

~~~~~

Baron Setford had watched with narrowed eyes as the Earl of Bentwick had greeted his bride-to-be. The man had shown about as much enthusiasm as a high society Lady might when asked to enter a pigsty. For a man receiving the honour of marrying a beautiful, and wealthy woman with a sizeable dowry, his manner was disrespectful, to say the least. Whilst Setford knew that Rotherhithe was simply doing what he thought best, to fulfil old Tillingford's last wishes, he wondered if Philip had made a serious misstep with this choice. It wasn't like him to misjudge so, but still...

Lady Georgiana looked remarkably unhappy, she barely touched her food, and she escaped the dining room as early as she politely could. He was a little worried about her. Gerald had noted him observing it all, and simply raised an enquiring eyebrow in his direction. Setford shook his head. They could discuss it later. He was, however, pleased to see, a short while later, that Miss Millpost, after a whispered few words with Lady Cordelia, had disappeared from the room. He presumed that she would see to Lady Georgiana.

As dinner concluded, and everyone retired to the grand salon for conversation and entertainment, he pulled Gerald aside for a moment in the hallway.

"I can't say that this is looking very positive. I don't think the girl likes Philip's choice for her at all. But, for now, let us simply spend the evening listening to the conversations amongst the unsuccessful suitors. With luck, and the application of sufficient brandy, something in their conversation may reveal more of the truth of the altercation with Dartworth."
~~~~~

The conversation, as the evening wore on, and the losing suitors drowned their sorrows in the Duke's excellent brandy, did become steadily more revealing.

One particular interchange between Bentwick and Eggmorton – the victims of Dartworth's attack - caught Setford's attention. Bentwick had dropped into the large window seat at the rear of the room, and Eggmorton joined him shortly thereafter.

"Eggmorton – must say, your jaw is still a rather ugly purple color where that scoundrel hit you. Is mine any better than yours?"

"No. If anything, I suspect your bruise is even more colourful than mine. Uncouth scum, that man! How were we to know that he would resort to physical violence – completely dishonourable. If he wanted to make a fuss, I'd expect a gentleman to call for a duel. Still – a bit hard to duel two of us at once, eh what?"

They laughed, the raucous laughter of men with too much drink in them, then swallowed their brandy with evident satisfaction. Bentwick, after what appeared to be a moments consideration, spoke again.

"And really, the hide of him. He had no claim to the girl, and was never likely to, so who does he think he is, to be objecting to what we said. Hmmph, those colonial commoners have addled the man's brain. He has no idea how to behave in society!"

Eggmorton nodded his vigorous agreement, and they dragged themselves to unsteady feet and went in search of more brandy.

Setford, having, the entire time, been seated beside Gerald, on a chaise not five feet from the men, concealed from their view by a rather extravagant potted palm, allowed himself to move, now that they had gone.

He met Gerald's eyes, and they both nodded. There was, as they had believed, something rather more to the story than the men had admitted to.

Given Bentwick's attitude to Lady Georgiana when the betrothal had been announced, this was a most disquieting situation – Setford was now quite certain that the man he had just overheard in conversation was not the kind of fellow that old Tillingford would have wanted for his daughter.

He wondered exactly what they had said, apparently about Lady Georgiana, that had been enough to bring Dartworth to violence.

<p style="text-align:center">~~~~~</p>

The following evening, as promised, the Duke held a truly magnificent ball.

A score of musicians had arrived in the late afternoon and the ballroom had been decked with bunting and the chandeliers sparkled with the light of hundreds of candles, the flickering light reflecting in the crystal wine glasses and hand carved crystal punch bowls.

The Duke formally called upon the guests to celebrate Lady Georgiana's betrothal and, eventually Georgiana had to submit herself to the ordeal of dancing a waltz with her newly-announced fiancé.

He held her far too tightly, trying to steer her like an unbroken horse through the whirling crowd of waltzing couples and, on more than one occasion he managed to step on her toes. She might not dance at all well, but she was not so clumsy as all that – with a man who knew how to guide her, she could just manage a passingly creditable waltz – although she avoided dancing as a general rule.

When she winced, the Earl scolded her for her clumsiness, even though the painful collision of his boot with her delicate dancing slipper was entirely his fault. Despite his pretensions, it was patently obvious that he was not an accomplished dancer.

"I see we shall have to whip you into shape, Georgiana," he snorted as he tried to steer her into a turn. "I'll be having none of your headstrong nonsense when you are my wife. You shall learn obedience and the virtue of keeping a still tongue in a wise head. You're not too old to be taught the lessons of the birch cane!"

Georgiana could scarcely believe what she was hearing. The arrogant pup, she thought. The birch cane? Why, she would soon make short shrift of this arrogant stripling of a man, and teach him the meaning of good manners!

"You smile at me, my Lady, in a way that I do not believe I like. Pray, what do you find so amusing in my company that it makes you smile so?"

"Why, my Lord, the thought of making sure that you truly get the wife you deserve makes me smile." He stepped on her toe and it was obviously deliberate. She winced but would not cry out. Instead, she kept the smile on her face, which failed to reach anywhere close to her beautiful eyes.

"You still have much to learn before you can match up to the title our marriage will confer on you, Georgiana. Much to learn. And I intend to be your tutor!"

As they passed the wide doorway to the ballroom, Georgiana turned lightly in the opposite direction to the Earls' urging, slipped easily out of his grasp, on through the double doorways and into the wide corridor that lay beyond.

She hated dancing. She could barely manage the most basic steps and dancing with a man with so little skill was enough to make them both a laughingstock should she permit the farce to continue. In that moment she decided, regardless of the fact that Cordelia and the Duke would undoubtedly be disappointed in her, to forsake the ghastly ball with its ghastly people and retire quietly to her chambers for the evening. Decision made, she rushed up the stairs with unseemly and very unladylike haste, only breathing a sigh of relief once her door was closed and locked behind her.

Chapter Nine

The calm solitude of her bedchamber was like a wonderful balm on her troubled soul. She sat wearily next to the fire that burned merrily in the hearth and watched the dancing flames as they curled and leapt gracefully around the logs that gave their warmth to the room. She had rapidly concluded that the young Earl was nothing more than an arrogant, self-serving, awful bore and her heart sank as she contemplated a lifetime of being trapped with such a deeply unpleasant man.

She must have dozed for a while, because she awoke with a start at the sound of someone knocking gently upon her door. She rubbed the sleep from her eyes and sat up.

"Who knocks at this hour?"

When the cheerful maid who daily prepared her hearth fire and kept her bedchamber in perfect order called to her through the door, she unlocked it and let her enter.

"What on earth brings you here at this time of the night?"

The maid curtsied and bowed her head. "Begging your pardon, your Ladyship, but I have something for you that I am charged to deliver only into your hands."

Georgiana took a sealed letter from the chambermaid's hands and the girl promptly turned on her heel and sped away like a shadow down the long corridor. Georgiana closed the door and locked it, before turning the letter over, not recognising the crest imprinted into the wax seal that held it closed. With one swift movement of her slender finger, she broke the seal and began to read.

The letter had been written by Oliver and brought to the chambermaid that very evening, by her sister who worked at the Inn, for delivery into Georgiana's hand. A moment later, she had to seek the support of her bed as she sat down to read the missive again and digest its importance.

"Lady Georgiana,

First and foremost, I must abjectly beg your forgiveness. I apologise profoundly for departing Canterwood Park without tendering to you an explanation. Given the Duke's direct order to leave his house, I found myself unable to delay. Honour and polite behaviour bound me to obey his order on the instant.

I cannot fault Rotherhithe for his actions in bidding me depart, for he was not present in the hallway to see or hear the events which led to my rather precipitate actions.

Therefore, it was understandable that he believed the lies he was told.

Yes, lies. I beg that you read on, and allow me to explain myself. I had settled myself on the chair in the hall, to brace myself a moment before joining the gentlemen in the Study. I was not looking forward to another evening as the target of their crude comments. As I sat there, a few of the men walked down the hall, conversing.

They were discussing you, in a manner which I found most impolite and offensive. The men doing most of the talking were Bentwick and Eggmorton. It was obvious to me that they had imbibed rather more of the Duke's fine wine and brandy than was, perhaps, wise, and that the drink had loosened their tongues.

I do not wish to shock or hurt you, but I believe it only fair that you know the truth of what they said.

They spoke spitefully, impugning your character and mocking what they claimed was your lack of manners. The Earl, in particular, made rather crude comments, to the effect that he would marry you, but only for the prize of your inheritance, for he declared, he would rather bed a common tavern girl than you, dear Lady Georgiana.

He described you as a wilful wench, a headstrong mare who should be whipped into obedience, for she behaved more like a stallion than a broodmare – which was all that a good wife should be.

They spoke on, becoming cruder and nastier as they went, until I could bear it no longer. How dare they speak so of you! For them, behaving as they were, to speak of you as having no manners was the darkest of humour to hear.

I simply could not stand by and hear such a buffoon, in silken breeches and a collar so high he could barely turn his head, besmirch you so.

I know that I am not a fit man to be a suitor for your hand, and that, therefore, I have no true right to be the defender of your honour, yet I could not bear to let it pass.

I do, most humbly apologise for interfering, but I simply could not allow it to pass. I stepped forth from the corner where I sat, and called upon the Earl to cease his foolish, untrue and offensive remarks.

He looked down his nose at me, and laughed in my face, calling me a crude peasant, then had the poor judgement to swing a fist at me.

I should have simply pushed it aside, for his inebriated state meant that he was not very accurate in his swing, but my reflexes took over.

I have, in the past, had need to defend myself, and my reactions were faster than my thoughts. I felled him with a solid punch to the jaw. Eggmorton then attempted to lay me out, with a punch from behind, and again, without though, I dealt with him in a similar manner. The fools lay on the floor wailing, and I stood, frozen with horror at what I had done, yet unable to truly regret it, as it was done in your defence.

At that moment, the Duke entered the hall, hearing the sounds of our altercation, and wrongly deduced that I had initiated the impromptu boxing bout. The other gentlemen, outraged to see two of their number laid low by a poorly dressed outsider, outbid one another in their loud condemnation, accusing me of starting the fight and demanding that the Duke set the dogs on me. If I had attempted to deny them, it would have been impossible – they would have claimed that I lied, and who would believe a paupered outsider over the cream of the *ton?*

So, at the Duke's stern behest, I reluctantly left the great house in disgrace.

I want to make absolutely clear to you, Lady Georgiana, that I only acted in defence of your honour and reputation. I could not bear the thought that you might think ill of me for my actions.

I am not proud of the violent manner in which I acted, yet I saw no other option in the moment.

I am, and always will be, your devoted servant, my Lady. And, should I be able to assist you in any way, I beg that you call upon me. I would face any disapprobation of the nobility in service to your honour.

Yours, always,

Oliver Kentworthy,

Marquess of Dartworth"

Georgiana let the letter drop into her lap. She shook her head to try to clear her thoughts. She didn't know whether to laugh or cry. As the tears sprang from her eyes she could not be entirely sure if they came from sadness or from joy. Or from both.

Chapter Ten

The Ball was drawing to a close when Georgiana finally emerged from her room. She had spent some time alternating between tears and laughter, her heart immeasurably lighter with the evidence that she had not, after all, so badly misjudged Oliver. In fact, she was feeling rather guilty about doubting him – she would need to apologise to him, when next she saw him – as she was determined to do, at the earliest opportunity.

She was feeling more composed now, although very angry at the insults and injustices that had taken place beneath the Duke's roof. The Earl of Bentwick had blackened her name and had compounded the injury by accusing Oliver of striking him without cause or provocation. If she had been a man, she would have taken a stout riding crop and whipped the young Earl for his falsehoods, or, better still, called him out in a duel. She would have boxed his ears and given him a sound thrashing. In the circumstances, he had escaped lightly with just a solid punch to the jaw and the indignity of being knocked to the floor.

Now that she had wiped the tears from her face, and made herself presentable, Georgiana ran, in a whirl of lace and petticoats, to find her sister.

Cordelia had spent evening dancing with almost every gentleman in the room. All of the nobility present had wanted to honour the soon-to-be Duchess of Rotherhithe by seeking her hand for a dance. Cordelia had relished every moment, revelling in the chance to show off her accomplishments as a finely tutored dancing partner. The Duke had spent the evening smiling broadly, proud to see his future bride's grace and beauty and knowing that many a man would envy him for his good fortune in wedding such a fine woman. He nodded at her as she passed his chair, whirling gracefully by with an elderly Marquess. Cordelia was born to the role. She was born to be a Duchess. Philip raised his glass of punch to her as she looked over the Marquess' stooped shoulder and smiled at her future husband.

As she took a welcome break and thought about how sore her poor feet were after a whole evening on the dance floor, Cordelia looked up and saw Georgiana standing alone in the grand doorway. She looked different this time, no longer troubled and sad, as she had looked earlier in the evening, worrying Cordelia. When Miss Millpost had informed Cordelia that Georgiana had fled to her room, she had not known whether to be relieved, or even more worried. She had not expected Georgie to return to the Ball.

Cordelia recognised the look on her face now. Georgiana was angry. She was holding something in her hand. A paper. A letter perhaps, and she signalled to her sister that she needed to speak to her. Outside the ballroom.

Cordelia curtsied to the Duke and asked permission to leave the ballroom for a few minutes to get some fresh air. The Duke laughed and implored her to return as quickly as possible for she was the sun that lit up the room and she would be leaving her poor guests in the miserable darkness of her absence. Cordelia smiled as she turned towards the doorway and quickly left the warm, stuffy, candlelit room behind her. Georgiana was waiting for her in the corridor. There was a fire in her eyes and a firmness in her jaw that spoke of a terrible, seething anger.

"Sister, what on earth has possessed you? You look as if you are ready to declare war upon the whole world!"

Georgiana proffered the letter.

"Read this and learn what could bestir me to so intense an anger."

Cordelia found a small, silk-covered chair next to a bright candelabra and sat to rest her weary feet and read the letter.

"My dear, this is from the Marquess Dartworth. How did he contrive to deliver a letter to this house when the Duke has forbidden him entrance?"

"Never mind how he spirited the letter into the house, Cordelia. Read what he has to say."

Cordelia's mouth opened and her jaw became slack as she digested the words. Her eyes moved across the well-formed characters and then her mouth tightened. She whispered the single word "Scoundrel!" even before she had finished the letter. She looked up at Georgiana. There were tears in her eyes. "You have been wronged, my dear. Grievously and unpardonably wronged."

Georgiana inclined her head in agreement.

"So, you can understand now why my temper has been so roused, can you not?"

"It's a ghastly situation and we must inform Philip of this development at the earliest opportunity."

Georgiana nodded, fully aware that all decisions would ultimately rest in the hands of the Duke.

"But we cannot disturb him with this news tonight. The Ball is almost over and we must leave him to play the gracious host until everyone has retired for the night. This news must wait until morning, my darling. Can you be patient and wait until breakfast?"

With another nod of the head, Georgiana accepted the wisdom of her sister's counsel. It would be rash to disturb the Duke in the midst of the celebrations. Better indeed to wait until the morning when clear heads and fresh coffee would aid in finding the best way forward.

Cordelia stood, wincing slightly from the tenderness of her feet and leaned forward to embrace her sister.

"You are in pain, Cordelia?"

"I have discovered that not every gentleman is dainty enough with his footwork to avoid stepping on my toes! But it's nothing. Now away to bed with you, and let us resolve to deal with this matter first thing in the morning."

Georgiana returned her sister's kiss and watched as she stepped lightly back into the ballroom, a gracious smile upon her pretty face, a perfect mask to disguise both her pain and her concern for her sister's future.

As she turned to return to her room, Georgiana felt her agitation slip away – if Cordelia could present a calm and gracious face until morning, so could she. At least now there was hope. Hope that she might not be doomed to a life with the Earl, at the very least, for, surely, after this revelation, the Duke would not force her to marry the odious man!

No one could be sure how the Duke would react to the letter's contents, but he prided himself upon being a man of fairness and honour, and Georgiana prayed that he would cleave to both virtues when he had the chance to read Oliver's letter in the light of day. Georgiana was only too aware that her entire future depended on it.

In spite of the stresses and excitements of the day, Georgiana slept deeply and well. No dreams came to disturb her rest and she awoke with the morning birdsong and felt as if a weight had been lifted from her chest. It was entirely possible that the Duke might not believe Oliver's version of events, but he would be duty bound to discover the truth. She found that notion deeply reassuring.

The Duke had risen early to take a small group of friends out into the fields with his prized falcons and he returned in excellent spirits. The sport gave him a healthy appetite and he was keen to break his fast with Cordelia at his side in the breakfast room.

As he sipped his coffee with eyes closed and a deep appreciation of the beverage's delicate flavours, Cordelia gently touched his arm and begged leave to show him something of importance.

The Duke opened his eyes and frowned at her.

"What is of such import that it needs to be seen before I have finished breaking my fast, my dear?"

"A letter, Philip. From the Marquess of Dartworth. A letter that you should read, regardless of what you think of the man."

"A letter from Dartworth, you say? What's this all about, my dear? You know the man's a scoundrel and a rogue. Is he begging for money? Hah! Nothing would surprise me less."

Cordelia passed the letter to her future husband.

"Philip, I would urge you to read what he has to say and reserve judgement until you have had seen what he has to say. And no, he is not begging for money. You will see that there is no advantage in this for him."

The Duke coughed lightly to display his evident scepticism, but he took the letter nonetheless, and began to peruse it, the bone china coffee cup poised halfway between lip and saucer. Within a few moments, the Duke frowned, pursing his lips and his face began to darken. He placed the cup carefully onto its saucer. He said nothing for a full two minutes. Then he summoned a footman with a hand gesture and told him to present his complements to the Earl of Bentwick, who was still sleeping after a surfeit of fine wine and cognac, and to invite him to attend upon the Duke in his study at ten that very morning. The Duke waved to another footman who hurried across to the table.

"Martin. Take a horse and ride post haste to the Bell and Whistle Inn and present my complements to the Marquess of Dartworth, who is lodging there. Ask him to attend upon me as my guest at the house this morning at ten. And make sure he understands that I mean ten of the hour and not a minute later."

The footman bowed and hurried off to the stables to find a fast mount.

Calling for yet another footman, the Duke asked that Baron Setford and Baron Tillingford be requested to attend upon him at nine of the morning. He owed Setford an apology, it seemed. Best get that out of the road first. Setford was a good man to have at your back, and would be of great assistance in ensuring that the truth was discovered. As would young Tillingford, he suspected, from what Setford had said of him. There were not many men that Setford treated with that sort of respect.

"Well my dear, we shall soon get to the bottom of this affair, and woe betide the man who has brought shame and lies into my house, whatever his rank and station may be!"

The Duke was about to leave the table, but Cordelia once more touched his sleeve and begged him to remain. "Philip, I fear that I have spoiled your appetite, and I ask your forgiveness. Pray stay with me a while longer and feed your strength. Coffee alone cannot sustain you! This injustice cannot go unrecognised. You will need something more substantial to fortify you for the events that seem likely to unfold."

The Duke could not help but smile. His future wife was the personification of grace and charm. How could he refuse her? He could see so clearly the love in her eyes.

"Very well, my dear. You have persuaded me! Let us revive our spirits with a good breakfast and feed the body as your presence feeds my very soul."

The footman rode at full speed, all the way to the Inn, which stood at the centre of the small, bustling community and dismounted swiftly, leaving his sweating horse with the ostler.

He removed his hat as he strode into the tavern, stamping his boots to warm his feet and give notice to the landlord that a visitor was waiting to be served.

"And what can we do for you on this fine March morning, young Martin?"

The innkeeper was a cheerful man, who had known Martin since he was a boy – and still rather saw him as one.

"I'll take a quart of ale, if you please, and would you send to the Marquess of Dartworth for I have a message for him from His Grace, the Duke."

The footman was halfway through his jug of ale when Oliver descended the stairs and asked why he had been disturbed. Martin relayed the Duke's message, impressing upon him how much importance the Duke had placed upon his timely attendance.

Oliver knew better than to ask further questions, as he was sure that the servant would be unlikely to be able to answer.

"My compliments to the Duke, and please inform him that I will be honoured to attend upon his pleasure at the stroke of ten."

The footman nodded, and drained his ale before heading out to his horse to ride back to the great house.

"Landlord? Do I have time for a hearty breakfast before I leave for the Duke's? You never know when such a meal may be a man's last!"

Oliver spoke lightly, but his humour was underlaid with an element of true concern.

The landlord nodded with a knowing look, all too aware of the capricious nature of many of the nobility, men who held the power of life and death over their tenants and others at times, simply because of the accident of their birth.

"Aye, Sir. A fine breakfast it will be. And if you are not certain of your return, you might want to settle your bill before you leave."

Oliver laughed.

"Of course. I would not leave this world as my father did with more debts than friends!"

"No offense, my Lord, but I do have a business to run and would surely grieve for you if anything amiss were to befall you. But I shall remember you more fondly when the account has been settled in full." The landlord smiled as he spoke, to take the potential sting from his words.

Oliver spilled a few silver coins across the counter and the landlord touched his balding head in appreciation of the gesture.

"Thank ye most kindly Sir. Now let us give you a fine breakfast to bid you God's speed and the hope that you may return in as good a health as you departed."

~~~~~

The footman found both Setford and Gerald to be awake and readied for the day, about to descend to break their fast. They, like the Duke, kept rather earlier hours than most of the nobility.
~~~~~

Setford merely nodded at the request, and assured the footman that they would present themselves to the Duke at the time that he had named.

He followed the footman into the upstairs corridor, and observed him make the same request of Gerald. Once the footman had left, he tapped on Gerald's door, and entered when bid.

"Well, Otford, what do you make of this then? I wonder what has the Duke in a bother this early in the morning? Perhaps he has thought better of his refusal to allow us to question Bentwick and Eggmorton further? Certainly, after hearing their conversation, I am utterly convinced that it is likely an injustice has been done here."

"I am completely in agreement with you there. I mislike this match between Bentwick and Lady Georgiana. She is obviously not best pleased with it, and Bentwick is colder to her than I have ever seen a man be to a woman he intends to wed. The Duke seems a good man, yet I fear he has sadly misjudged this situation. Still, perhaps this summons indicates that something new has come to light, that has changed his views?"

"I would hope so, m'boy, but I don't hold too much hope. Rotherhithe can be a stubborn man. This summons to attend upon him may be related to something else entirely."

"True, regardless, if we wish to break our fast before we speak with him, we'd best be about it."

Setford nodded in agreement, and they took themselves off to the breakfast room, each pondering the possibilities inherent in the day.

~~~~~

When Setford and Gerald entered the Duke's Study, they found him seated at his desk, a serious expression on his face and a letter in his hand.

"Gentlemen, I trust you are in good health this morning? Please, be seated – I have need of your opinion and support."

"I assure you that we are both in far better health than most of your guests who, I fear, rather overindulged in your excellent wines last night."

Setford chuckled as he spoke, quite certain that most of the young fops were still abed, nursing sore heads from the effects of copious quantities of spirits. The Duke nodded, but his face remained serious. Interesting – Setford wondered what it was that needed their 'opinion and support'.

"Setford, old friend, I must start this conversation by offering you an apology. When you came to me, after the altercation with Dartworth, and asked to question the situation further, I fear that I was rather pig-headed. I should know better. In all the years that we have known each other, you have rarely questioned my judgement. And never without good reason. I should have listened to you."

Setford smiled, waving the apology aside.

"Rotherhithe, you need not apologise. You are entitled to your own opinions, and to be stubborn about them. But, in this case, I sense that something has happened to bring you to make this apology? Something beyond a sudden recognition of your own stubbornness?"
~~~~~

"Indeed, you are correct. This is what has happened."

He indicated the letter, which was still grasped in his hand, and passed it to Setford.

"If you would, gentlemen, please read the contents of that letter, and then give me the benefit of your opinion on it. I am inclined to believe it wholly truth, but I intend to prove that a little later this morning, with your assistance, should you agree."

For some minutes, there was no sound in the room, beyond the loud tick of the elegant clock on the mantle, as Setford read the missive, then passed it, without comment, to Gerald. Once Gerald had read it, and passed it back to the Duke, Setford spoke.

"I am unsurprised, Rotherhithe. And, in fact, I believe that Otford here, and I can corroborate what's said in that letter for you. The night before last, in the salon after dinner, we happened to overhear a conversation between Bentwick and Eggmorton. A conversation in which they discussed the events of the altercation. I believe that Bentwick's exact words to Eggmorton were: *'And really, the hide of him. He had no claim to the girl, and was never likely to, so who does he think he is, to be objecting to what we said. Hmmph, those colonial commoners have addled the man's brain. He has no idea how to behave in society!'* Words which, I believe, make it rather clear that what Dartworth has said in that letter is likely the whole truth."

"Setford, you always have had the most astounding memory! I have no doubt that is exactly what you heard the man say. Otford, do you agree with Setford's memory?"

"Indeed, I do, Your Grace."

The Duke nodded with satisfaction.

"Then, gentlemen, may I ask you to attend upon me here, a short while from now, just before the hour of ten. I have summoned both Bentwick and Dartworth here. I will have the truth of it from Bentwick's own mouth, and I would appreciate you being witness to the whole conversation, that, later, none may doubt what I do or say."

They both stood, and bowed.

"As you wish, Your Grace – we are at your disposal. I do, however, faced with that prospect for the morning, feel the need for another cup of your excellent coffee to fortify myself."

The Duke, feeling rather lighter of heart than before the conversation, laughed aloud. Setford had the reputation amongst his friends as a connoisseur of coffee, with the magical ability to ensure its availability in any circumstance – so his complimenting the coffee was a considerable honour. Philip would have to remember to tell Juan of the accolade to his coffee making, once the house full of guests had departed.

~~~~~

The mantle clock ticked quietly and revealed the hour at two minutes to ten. The Duke consulted his gold pocket watch as he sat calmly behind his carved and inlaid desk, his hands steepled and a glass of madeira at his side. Setford and Gerald sat quietly to one side, where they would not immediately be obvious to a person entering the room. There was a light knock at the door and a servant bowed as he made way for the Earl of Bentwick.
~~~~~

"Your Grace, I am most honoured by your invitation to attend upon you, but in faith, it is an uncommonly early hour to be up and about."

The Duke detected the odour of stale wine upon the Earl's breath and grimaced, nodding slowly.

"We have matters to discuss, Bentwick, and the hour will not wait."

"if it is about Lady Georgiana's dowry, I have already made preparations to place one of my men as overseer and make sure that the land is exploited to the utmost. There are too many idle hands on the estate and I aim to see a handsome profit from better farming and fewer mouths to feed. You would agree with me, I assume, Your Grace?"

The Duke pursed his lips, finding the blatant greed inherent in the man's words rather tasteless.

"That is not the subject of our meeting, Bentwick. We have more serious matters to examine. Questions of honour."

He left the word hanging in the air between them as the young Earl shifted uneasily in his seat.

"Honour, Your Grace? What in heaven's name has my honour to do with this invitation to meet, a courteous gathering of men of breeding and nobility?"

"Everything. And nothing. We shall soon see."

As the clock struck the hour of ten, there was another gentle knock at the study door and Dartworth, with muddied boots and flecks of horse sweat on his tail coat, entered the room, standing tall above the two other men. Bentwick had not yet noticed the presence of Setford and Gerald.

Dartworth, obviously a more observant man, noted their presence, and simply raised an eyebrow in their direction, enquiringly. Setford shook his head, and indicated that Dartworth should concentrate his attention on the Duke and Bentwick.

Oliver turned back, to see the Earl of Bentwick sit back in surprise and stammer, some anger in his tone, "What is this rogue doing in this house, Your Grace? He has no business to be here. Did you not cast him forth, bidding him not return?"

The Duke studied the two men before him carefully.

"The Marquess is here at my invitation, Bentwick. At this moment, he is my guest."

The Duke invited Oliver to sit, indicating a comfortable chair, opposite the Earl near the Duke's great mahogany desk.

"Now, gentlemen," the Duke leaned forward. "Let us discover the truth of what took place in my house. Let us see who speaks the truth and who has spoken lies under my roof. I will have the truth of it, gentlemen, so help me God."

Carefully unfolding the letter, the Duke began to read its contents, looking up occasionally at the two men seated before him. The Earl was looking distinctly nervous, visibly squirming in his seat. Oliver was calm, impassive, coolly appraising the Earl and clearly prepared to administer another blow to the man's foolish head if the occasion demanded it. He was not certain of the Duke's intent, but, if Lady Georgiana had willingly entrusted the letter to him, surely there was some hope of a fair outcome. It seemed unlikely that the man would have invited him here, like this, if he intended to disregard the contents of the letter.

At length, the Duke reached the end of the letter and pointed at the Earl.

"Now, my Lord, what do you have to say?"

"It's all nonsense! This man is a liar, a cheat, a thief and a rogue. You cannot believe a single word that he says."

Oliver leaned forward in his chair, his hands still on his knees.

"You besmirch my honour, my Lord, as you have besmirched the honour of a Lady whom I esteem far beyond the value of your miserable life."

A terrible silence fell upon the room as the words sank in. This was not some idle tavern insult over tankards of ale.

Oliver continued. "I do not demand an apology from you, my Lord, for your words are quite meaningless. I demand the satisfaction of your blood to wash away the stain of your insults."

The Earl blanched. The Duke was visibly shocked. This was entirely unexpected. He quickly gathered his wits.

"Pray, gentlemen, we do not need to come to such a remedy. We have not had a duel in these parts for some five years and I would not countenance such an event today. My wedding day is nigh upon us and I will not have the ceremony blighted by the spilling of blood!"

"Honour has its price, Your Grace, and this gentleman has called mine into question, as well as the honour of Lady Georgiana. His words have created a debt. Now he must settle his account." There was an ominous pause as Oliver stared hard at the trembling aristocrat. "An account that must be settled with me."

"Now stay your words for a moment, Dartworth. Let us not act in haste." The Duke turned towards the visibly shaken young Earl. "Think hard before you speak. I ask you again - what have you to say for yourself, Bentwick?"

The Earl stammered. He was perspiring around his lace collar and beads of sweat had appeared on his forehead.

"Look here, Dartworth. I did not mean any offense to you or the good Lady." He wrung his hands in a nervous display of obvious concern for his personal safety. "We were joking. Perhaps we'd had a little too much brandy. In heaven's name. It was a jest. A poor jest. Nothing more." Oliver continued to stare at him, his expression hard. "Dartworth, you must believe me when I express my regrets. Please, my Lord, accept my apology, let us shake hands like good sports and be done with the matter."

The Duke nodded gravely.

"So you admit that Dartworth is telling the truth here?"

"Well, errr, I may have said a few of those things, but, as I said, it was only meant in jest."

"You described Lady Georgiana as a headstrong mare that needed to be whipped into obedience?"

"Heavens above, Your Grace. I cannot remember every foolish quip and comment I might have made!"

"This is a most serious matter, my Lord, and your answers cannot be couched in vague half-truths and deceptions. It is either a yes or a no, and I demand that you speak plainly."

The Earl fell silent as the mantle clock ticked quietly in the background.

"I favour the sabre as a duelling weapon," said Oliver quietly. "I have used it on many occasions and would deem it the best means to accept redress from a man."

The Earl's head shot up.

"Sabres, you say?"

He could not help but take stock of the Marquess's powerful build, the muscled shoulders and strong arms that would wield a blade so cruelly and effectively.

"Yes, my Lord. The sabre. The perfect means to flay your hide and carve fillets from your limbs."

To the Earl's horror, Oliver smiled at this point and the wide grin sent chills down his spine. Setford fought to repress a laugh at the sight of the man's face. Dartworth was doing an excellent job of acting the ferocious and dangerous killer.

"Very well! If you would have me confess, I admit it. I spoke those words. It is all true. Lady Georgiana is unmannered and not worthy of my family name. I accepted the betrothal only for her prize of her estate. There! Now you have it. Are we done now?"

Oliver shook his head slowly.

"No, Sir. We are not done. You still owe me a full measure of your skin for the dishonour that you have cast upon me, as well as upon the Lady Georgiana, I will have it tomorrow at dawn upon the heath, and there you shall learn the price of your treachery."

"For pity's sake, my Lord!" whined the Earl. "You cannot press this demand for vengeance. I am an Earl and I will not be trifled with!"

"Then you shall be buried as an Earl and your lands and titles will not save you upon the morrow."

"No!" screamed the Earl. "It cannot be!"

The Duke sighed.

"I am afraid it can, Bentwick. The rules of honour give the Marquess the right to demand satisfaction. I do not approve of it, but you must choose a second to accompany you and prepare yourself to meet Dartworth at sunrise tomorrow. May God have mercy upon your soul."

The Earl broke into tears and sobbed, sinking to the floor and imploring Dartworth to forgive him. The sight of a grown nobleman grovelling so quite turned the Duke's stomach – had this man no courage at all, no sense of honour? Of a certainty, choosing this man as a mate for Georgiana had been one of the worst decisions of his life. Thank God, he had discovered the truth in time.

"So, my Lord, your honour has come to this?" Oliver looked down at the man crying at his feet. "You would prefer to live in shame and disgrace than die as a man defending your honour?"

"Please, my Lord. I beg you. Have pity on me. I do not wish to die."

Oliver stood and moved to the wide fireplace, which held a glowing pile of small logs which spread warmth into the Study. He considered the situation for a few minutes without speaking. Setford and Gerald watched with interest. The Duke remained silent, contemptuous of the Earl's appalling lack of courage and character. The arrogant whelp certainly deserved a whipping, but the Duke did not feel that he deserved to die.

Oliver finally turned towards the young man, who was still weeping and grovelling on the rug before him.

"Perhaps we can put a price on your honour after all, Bentwick."

The Duke considered the Marquess with shrewd eyes.

"What are you proposing, Dartworth?"

"A private arrangement. An equitable resolution. Since the Earl has far more money than honour, I propose that we put a fair price on this day's business and let him weigh out his worth in gold pieces."

"You mean blood money, Dartworth? Rather an unconventional solution for a matter of honour between gentlemen, but, as Bentwick has proven himself to be somewhat lacking in conventional honour, perhaps that is outstandingly appropriate." The Duke struggled to keep a straight face as he spoke. This was better than he could ever have hoped for. "A bargain in return for the Earl's honour and reputation?"

Oliver nodded in agreement.

"Yes, Your Grace. My father squandered my inheritance and, through no fault of my own, I have been reduced to labouring and toiling to keep body and soul together, to have some hope of restoring my estate and doing right by my tenants. I would as soon put an end to this miserable dog's life with my sabre, and know that honour had been duly satisfied, but this may be Providence's way of putting my affairs to rights."

The Duke nodded.

"What do you have to say, Bentwick? Will your father's money be sufficient to keep that fine hide of yours securely upon your back, or would you prefer to take the gentlemanly way out, and meet Dartworth at dawn upon the morrow to take your chances with a sabre?"

"I'll pay! By heaven, I'll pay!" squealed the Earl. "And let not a word of this spread beyond this room, I beg of you."

Oliver asked leave to write a note of agreement with the Duke's fine quill pen and the Earl of Bentwick was only too happy to add his signature to the contract that was duly witnessed and sealed with the Duke's own hand.

"Setford, Otford, if you would. I would have you witness this too, that there is no doubt of what has been said, done, and agreed here this day."

The Earl spun around in horror at realising that his spineless behaviour had been witnessed by others. He dropped his face into his hands as the other two men stepped forward, and signed as witness to his contract.

"This agreement is both legal and binding. I can assure both of you that, should you try to question it, the ruling will always go in favour of the Marquess. I am well connected in the highest levels of the legal profession, and beyond. I suggest that you do not consider anything other than full compliance with what has been agreed." Setford's voice was cold, and his piercing grey eyes held the Earl's until the younger man looked away.

"Bentwick, you have thirty days to deliver the agreed sum to the Marquess or you have my pledge that you will be exposed in public, and in private, as a scoundrel and a rogue. Now leave this chamber, pack your bags and leave my house."

As the Earl departed the Study, the Duke beckoned Oliver to a chair.

"You will take a glass of madeira with me, Dartworth?"

"It would be an honour, Your Grace."

The two men sipped their small glasses of the sweet wine and soaked in the warmth of the crackling logs. This year, the spring was late arriving, the frosts were still unseasonably thick, and the warmth was welcome.

"Dartworth? I must ask you something of a personal nature and I would value your candour."

Oliver nodded. "Certainly. I will answer honestly and truthfully."

"I thought you would. Now tell me plainly, was it your intention to put the Earl into the perilous position where he would have no choice but to offer you a king's ransom in return for his life?"

Oliver laughed out loud which surprised the Duke.

"Your Grace, I enjoy the game of chess as much as any man but I had no intention of playing the Earl for a pawn in some grand game of strategy!"

"You did not intend to hold a blade to his throat to persuade him to part with his purse?"

"Heavens and by my faith, no, your Grace. That was never my intention. I wanted to teach the pup a lesson for treating Lady Georgiana so poorly. I admit that his comments angered me and his greed appalled me."

The Duke nodded his agreement to that sentiment.

Oliver continued, "But it was only when he was begging upon your floor that the idea came to me that he might be of better service to my needs as a willing donor of gold coin than as a fashionably dressed corpse!"

The Duke laughed.

"By all that's holy, Dartworth, the look on the wretch's face was surely beyond price. Egad, but if you hadn't called him out for a duel, I would've whipped him myself with the stoutest birch rod in the county."

"It seems appropriate to me that my father's fortune, which was squandered on gambling amongst the gentry, has now been restored as the result of the bringing to justice of just the sort of greedy and unthinking young nobleman who once drove my father to ruin."

The Duke laughed.

"Just so, Dartworth. Just so. We can announce to the world that what was lost through folly has been restored through prudence. Did your father really lose so much as the amount you have extracted from the fool?"

"Not quite so much, Your Grace, but the debts are but the start of it. He left the entailed properties in appalling condition, due to long term lack of maintenance. My estate needs repairs and investment and I decided to add a goodly interest to the sum to make up for my lean and hard years of toil."

"It might not have been fitting labour for a gentleman, Dartworth, but it has not diminished you one bit. You are a true gentleman through and through. I must offer you my sincere apology for every doubting you."

The Duke leaned forward and offered his hand to the Oliver.

"You will stay for the wedding? It is set to be but a week from now, and I would be honoured if I may provide you with more fitting attire to attend the occasion, for you will have little chance to arrange new things of your own in time. You are a Marquess, my Lord, and I would have you dressed and attired as such."

Oliver smiled and showed his even white teeth, more pleased than he could possibly say to accept the Duke's generous hospitality.

Within a short hour, the entire household had learned that Lady Georgiana's engagement to the young Earl had been cancelled. There were few explanations given, but the Duke had taken great care to explain as much as he could to Georgiana, his future wife seated by his side, and a carafe of the finest madeira to fortify their spirits and soften the shock of the dramatic events.

Georgiana felt as if a stone had finally been lifted from her heart. Despite the seriousness of the conversation, she could not stop smiling at the Duke's words. In her minds eye, she saw Oliver, as he had looked when the Duke had ordered him from the house, those few short days ago. In that moment, she wanted, desperately, to see him, to make certain that the sadness was gone from his eyes, and to apologise to him for ever having believed him anything but honourable.

With a start, she realised that she had been woolgathering, and that the Duke was still speaking. When she brought her attention back to his words, her smile grew even larger, on the instant.

"You shall be entirely free henceforth to choose a husband of your own pleasing, my girl. That might mean you will be my guest here for longer than either of us originally planned. The house is yours for as long as you wish and you are free to take your pick of any of the horses in the stables and go riding whenever the fancy takes you. And to amuse yourself with the puppies – although I'd prefer you didn't bring them to the house! You see, your sister has told me more about you than you might've expected!"

Georgiana accepted the Duke's kiss upon her hand as he stood to leave the room. He turned to face the two Ladies.

"Now, if the rumours can be believed, we have a wedding to attend here in a very short time so let us put all our hearts into the joyous occasion and put the past firmly behind us, where it belongs."

Georgiana raised her exquisitely carved glass of madeira in a toast.

"To your happiness, my darling sister, for there is truly no one in the world who deserves it more than you."

They smiled at each other as their glasses chimed together and the lead crystal rang out clearly like a small, perfect bell in the confines of the study.

~~~~~

Later that day, Baron Setford managed to catch the Duke alone, for a private word. After his observations of the last few days, an idea had started to form and this time he wanted the Duke's opinion.
~~~~~

"Rotherhithe, we've been friends for many years now. You are, perhaps, more aware of what I do than most men. What you may never have considered is how wide is the scope of my remit, in the work that I carry out for the crown."

"I can't say I've ever thought too deeply on it. After all, for most of the years you've done that work, the main focus has been France, the war on their soil, and the risk of their action and infiltration here. It seems so obvious that it's only now, when you mention it, that I have realised that, perhaps you look further than that."

"And glad I am that most have never considered what I do, or how far it reaches. In this case though, I feel it appropriate to inform you a little further. In strictest confidence, of course."

"Of course."

"My remit stretches to all areas of the world where there is an English presence, or a diplomatic... challenge... for us. Including the Americas. I also prefer, when I can, to have a direct hand in recruiting those who work for me, in whatever guise. I am certain that you have realised that young Otford is one of those. He, and his close friends, were some of our most effective men in France. I value his opinion."

The Duke nodded again, wondering where this was going.

"And both he and I have come to the conclusion that young Dartworth's connections in America, and his knowledge of the political workings of the place, could be of great value to the crown. I've a mind to offer him an opportunity. Do you think he would consider it? For, whilst the *ton* have labelled him a revolutionary, my sense of it is that, at the heart of it, he's loyal."

Rotherhithe sat a moment, considering Setford's words, before he spoke again.

"I believe that I agree with you. He has some rather challenging opinions, but they are not, by any means, rash or unconsidered. He is not the sort of revolutionary that wants to destroy the aristocracy, or our way of life. Rather, from what I see, he would seek to make quiet changes that benefit everyone, where he can. He certainly acknowledges his responsibility for his tenants and his estates. Yet he undoubtedly has conceived some sympathy for the American people. Perhaps, I could dare to surmise, he understands them better than most in England might. What would you offer him?"

"The peace with the Americans is still fragile, and the risk of military action resulting from some minor stupidity along the current border between British North America and the United States is high. Both the Prince Regent and the Parliament would prefer that not happen. Perhaps a new treaty may be possible, to resolve such questions in a better manner. But... I would be much more comfortable if our negotiators were *extremely* well informed, should such negotiations come to pass. And that requires the kind of intelligence that can only be gathered by someone there, who already has contacts, and knows his way around. If Dartworth would consider a journey to the Americas, in the near future, I feel that it could be most beneficial. I am, however, aware that I will need to provide good and convincing reason for his travel, as well as the best of support for the management of his properties here, in his absence."

The Duke nodded, his face serious, considering all of the implications of Setford's words.

"I think that he might well accept such a mission. It seems to me that facilitating a treaty between his home country, and the country whose people he respects for their achievements, would suit his attitudes well. But… give him some time before you ask. Let's see how he settles. He seemed to get on well with Otford, so let us encourage that friendship – Otford is astute enough to discover, for you, how Dartworth might really feel about such a request from you."

"True, a good way forward I think, Rotherhithe. And now I will leave you in peace, after the dramas of the day, to contemplate the much more pleasant prospect of your impending wedding."

Chapter Eleven

The following week was a whirlwind of activity as the household prepared for the Duke's wedding. Linen for the banqueting tables was carefully unfolded and perfectly ironed, silver cutlery was polished until it shone brightly, cases of fine wine were unpacked and the corks checked for a perfect seal. Boxes of snuff from faraway Turkey were gently opened and twists of Virginia tobacco were finely hand-shredded for smoking.

Lead crystal decanters were cleaned and set ready to receive Cognac that had been aged in oak casks for twenty years and fresh candles were trimmed and placed in the scores of candelabra and chandeliers for which the great house was justly famous.

The kitchens prepared for the effort of boiling up and crystallising a massive quantity of sugar to make exquisite decorations to adorn the tables. It was to be an event that would be talked of for years to come.

Everyone pretended not to notice the Earl of Bentwick's sudden absence, and, whilst the rules of polite society deterred the guests from discussing the Earl's affairs, at least in public, much gossip was whispered in quiet corners, as they all speculated on the events which had led to his sudden departure. Rumours, of course, abounded. Servants whispered to chambermaids and footmen exchanged comments behind gloved hands and, before long, the personal maids were sharing the gossip with their mistresses.

Whilst the Earl's humiliation had been private, when he had begged for his life rather than face a duel over a Lady's honour, rumour speculated on what had actually happened. The common thread was that the man was, in some way, an utter scoundrel and a rogue! Given the intensity of the gossip, the Duke thought it likely that, unless he was able to convince those with influence to overlook his indiscretions, he would soon find the doors of the *ton*'s great houses firmly barred against him. Invitations to glittering social events would no longer be extended. The Earl would sink into the kind of social obscurity that felt more like a slow and lingering death and, ostracised by his fellow peers, he would likely turn to his cellars to find solace and comfort, a drunken sot without a friend to call upon. The Duke could not find it in himself to feel sorry for the man.

To the guests who had assembled in all of their finery to celebrate the Duke's wedding, the Earl had ceased to be important, except as the occasional subject of titillating gossip. The Duke's wedding was of far more interest. Although, there was still some quiet speculation as to which gentleman might now hope to win Lady Georgiana's hand.

Those who had sulked and retreated into cards and drinking, when her betrothal had been announced, now put effort into charming her, hoping that they might step into the place that the Earl had vacated.

Oliver had retained his rooms at the local tavern. The Duke had been more than happy to extend the hospitality of his house to the Marquess, but Oliver quickly realised that his rooms at the Bell and Whistle Inn were undoubtedly larger and more accommodating than the ones that were available at Canterwood Park. With so many other guests already in residence, the Duke could only offer the lesser bedchambers to any late invitations and Oliver had politely declined the offer of occupying what was little more than a garret in the building's attics.

His only regret in staying at the Inn was that it gave him less opportunity to see Lady Georgiana. Shortly before he had left the house again, in a much better frame of mind than the last time that he had passed out that door, he had seen Georgiana in the hallway, as she came from the Duke's study with her sister. He had smiled hesitantly, going forward to bow over her hand, and been utterly delighted when her face had lit with a brilliant smile.

Perhaps there was hope for him yet – for now, with his fortunes, if not completely restored, at least in a decent, and soon to be debt free, state, he might reasonably approach her as a suitor.

The Duke had been as good as his word and had sent Oliver a wardrobe of fine clothing to befit his station as the Marquess of Dartworth.

It was fortunate, indeed, that the Duke was almost of a size with Oliver, although some of the clothing he had, regretfully, been unable to accept, as it was simply unable to accommodate his breadth of shoulder. Oliver reasoned that almost anything would have been an improvement on his old clothes and was delighted to be able to dress as befit a gentleman. He cared little for fashion but, amongst the *ton*, clothes were, too often, the way a man was valued.

Oliver found himself laughing. If anything, the clothing was probably a little too fine for his more modest tastes. These were the silver-buttoned coats, the finely-embroidered shirts, and the silken breeches of a Duke, after all. He had spent so long toiling for his living in the former colonies that he'd almost forgotten what it was like to dress in such expensive finery.

Furthermore, he had absolutely no idea what such clothing cost – it was so long since he had been able to consider the extravagance of a good tailor. Oliver was, however, quite certain that the value of the clothing gifted to him was enormous, and he deduced that the Duke was endeavouring to make amends for his poor judgement. He appreciated the gesture and determined to offer his thanks and his respects at the earliest opportunity.

Each day, he dressed in his new finery with care, and took himself to Canterwood Park. Whilst the gathered cream of high society still eyed him somewhat askance, the Duke's changed attitude to him had caused a softening in their manner. They were, he understood, also absolutely curious about what had brought about his obvious change in fortunes.

The days were, in contrast to his previous time in the house, a delight. He walked in the gardens with Lady Georgiana, Miss Millpost following at a discreet distance. They talked of everything and nothing. He shared his plans for the renovation of Dartworth Abbey, and the transformation of his tenant farmers lives and productivity. Georgiana was filled with enthusiasm and ideas, providing excellent advice. He was again, astounded by her sharp intelligence and her care for the land. In her presence, he quite forgot everything, and everyone else.

Yet he had not dared to raise the question of her future. For now, just the chance to be with her would have to be enough.

When he was not spending time with Lady Georgiana, he found himself often in the company of Baron Tillingford. Gerald had quickly told him to dispense with formality, and they also spoke of land and property, and the challenge of dealing with the *ton*.

There was something about Gerald that reminded him of himself. A sense of sadness, a sense of feeling out of place. He did not ask, but he was sure that there were things in Gerald's past that the man regretted. Regardless of that, Oliver quickly decided that this was a man he wanted as a friend, for he had not been, even at first meeting, judgemental – he had accepted Oliver for himself, and that was something to be treasured.

Increasingly, also, he found himself in conversation with Baron Setford. A disconcerting man, with those piercing grey eyes, and the ability to almost disappear from notice, even in a crowded room. But a man, he discovered, with a sharp sense of humour, and an equally sharp sense of loyalty and honour.

A man, it seemed, who was dangerous to cross, but who had decided, for his own reasons, to be Oliver's friend. He was grateful, but wondered what the Baron saw in him.

~~~~~

"… but the entire roof will need repair before the place is reasonably habitable. I have no idea at all how my father managed to live there, in the end."

Georgiana watched the animation in Oliver's face as he spoke. His eyes were bright, and his unruly dark curls shone in the sun. She found herself wanting to reach out and touch him. Even while her mind was engaged in the enthusiastic discussion of his plans for restoring his estates, her body seemed to be drawn towards him, all of its own.

"Will you restore it all? Surely that will be a great expense?"

"I will, for it is my heritage. It's an entailed property, so really, I have no choice but maintain it. It would be most uncouth of me to let it rot, when I shall be forced to pass it on to my son. Should I have a son, of course."

Georgiana thought that Oliver actually blushed as he said those words, but he quickly turned away, to stare out across the beautiful grounds of Canterwood Park, as he continued speaking.

"And I want to. I want to see it returned to the beautiful place it was, when I was a small child. I want to see my tenants happy, their cottages in good repair, the lands productive. I want them to be happy to see me – as they certainly never were to see my father. Is that selfish of me?"
~~~~~

"No, oh no, never selfish, for to achieve what you wish, you will improve the lives of many others. Not just your tenants, but all those who you employ to do the repairs, and all those that they support, or spend their money with. That is far more generous than most titled men ever are in their thinking."

They walked on, coming to a little stone folly that sat amongst a cluster of trees, with a view to the hills. Georgiana dropped onto the seat, impulsively reaching out to pull Oliver down beside her.

He sat. She did not release his hand. She did not, in that moment, care in the slightest if she was being terribly forward, or totally inappropriate. His fingers felt good in hers. His hand was strong, warm, calloused from his years of honest work, and gentle, as his fingers curled to press against hers.

Her heart seemed to have decided to beat at double its normal pace, when he turned and met her eyes. She was lost. The world around them disappeared. There was only his face. He looked at her with wonder, as if she were the most precious thing he had ever seen.

He had spent all week with her, walking, talking, laughing. But never saying the words she wanted to hear. Never asking her of her plans, now that her betrothal to the odious Earl of Bentwick was over, now that she could choose for herself.

Did he still wish to court her, as he had said in their first real conversation, all those weeks that seemed forever ago? Did her care for her? She hoped that he did.

For she had discovered that she cared for him, rather intensely.

This week, she had come to live for the moments in his company, and could not, truth to tell, imagine, now, a time when she would not have his company.

Her sister's wedding was tomorrow.

Once it was over, Oliver would leave – would go to Dartworth Abbey and begin to enact the plans they had discussed. If she did nothing, he might leave without either of them ever saying how they felt. Georgiana could not bear the thought. She had always been the brave, and somewhat outrageous one. Perhaps it was time to be outrageous again.

"Oliver?"

"Yes, Georgiana?"

His voice was warm, her name a caress on his lips. She shivered slightly, and took a deep breath.

"Oliver… I… do not wish you to leave, after the wedding." She felt foolish, the words all wrong. "Oh. That's sounds not as I mean it at all! Of course I wish you to go to Dartworth Abbey, and to do all of the wonderful things that we have spoken of. But… I will miss you, I will miss our conversations. I… I am trying to say that I care for you."

Suddenly embarrassed, blushing, and wondering if she had made a terrible mistake, Georgiana went to turn her head away. Oliver reached up, and cupped her cheek in his palm, turning her gently back to face him. Softly, his lips met hers, and she felt herself dissolve against him as her whole body flooded with warmth.

Minutes later, they drew apart, each with an expression of dazed wonderment.

"Georgiana... I... should not have done that. But I do not regret it in the least. I have wanted to do that, almost from the first moment that I saw you. Thank you. Thank you for being braver than I, and telling me of your feelings. I am a fool – for I should have told you of my feelings long ago, but fear that you might reject me, as too crude and uncouth, like so many others have, held me back. No more. Georgiana, I care for you too, more deeply than you can imagine. May I... may I presume to court you, my Lady?"

"Oh please, do! Of all the men gathered here to try to woo me, you are the only one who ever interested me in the slightest. Let us begin as if all of the nightmare moments of the last few weeks had never happened, and see how, in truth we might feel about each other, when others opinions are not intruding."

Oliver's face lit with a smile, and he looked, Georgiana thought, more handsome than ever. He drew her to him again, kissing her gently, but with a simmering heat of passion quivering beneath the surface. He drew back, breathing hard, still smiling as if he would never stop, then pulled her to her feet, beginning to walk back towards the house, her hand still clasped in his.

"You have just made me happier than I have been for a very, very long time. I will do the right thing, and formally ask the Duke for his approval of me courting you – I know that he has given you the right to your own choice, but it is the honourable thing to do, to at least tell him!"

"As you wish, Oliver."

They reached Miss Millpost, who sat on a stone bench amongst the hedges, and she looked at them, took in their wide smiles, then pointedly looked down to their joined hands, and raised an eyebrow silently. Georgiana laughed and Oliver released her hand, laughing too. Miss Millpost, after a moment, joined in their merriment, then, restoring her 'official chaperone' face, escorted them back into the house, walking a suitable, and duly proprietous, distance apart.

~~~~~

The day of the wedding was blessed with sunshine, which was warm and pleasant, even given the unseasonably cold spring. Birds chattered in the trees and dipped their beaks in the bird baths that decorated the extensive gardens. There were even a few flowers finally blooming, scenting the light breeze. Georgiana woke before the dawn, eager to be with her sister on this wonderful day and to do everything she could to be of help.

Cordelia had loved her and cared for her throughout her entire life and now at last she could do something to repay that endless generosity and nobility of spirit.

Cordelia had maids a-plenty to help her, but Georgiana insisted on joining in, adding flourishes to her sister's hair and applying the delicate make-up that would enhance her features and make everyone nod and smile with unabashed approval.

"We should engage an artist to capture your image in oils, my dear," giggled Georgiana as she added just a tiny touch more rouge to her sister's cheeks.

"What? And sit for my portrait for hours and hours on end? Why, I would miss my own wedding!"
~~~~~

The wedding dress had been sewn from a heavy silk brocade and patterned with hundreds of crystals and tiny pearls. The rich ivory fabric, which held just the softest blush of gold in its colour, set off Cordelia's dark hair and pale skin to perfection. It was simply breath-taking. There was a veil, crafted from the finest, almost transparent muslin, pierced with the most delicate embroidery and edged with beautiful lace, to be draped to fall elegantly from where it was pinned into her hair.

Cordelia would look like a classical goddess from the ancient myths and legends, a vision of loveliness and Georgiana thought her heart would burst with pride and pleasure at her sister's obvious happiness.

At half past the hour of ten in the morning, with sunlight streaming in through the stained-glass windows of the beautiful old church in the village of Canterwood Downs, Philip Canterwood stood proudly and placed a simple gold band upon Cordelia's finger.

At the speaking of the vows, the couple were bound together in holy matrimony and ladies of rank wept openly at the beauty of the simple ceremony. Even one of the elderly Earls found himself blowing heavily into his kerchief to disguise the tears that had clouded his eyes, suddenly mindful of his distant days as a newly-wedded bridegroom.

The Duke was beaming at his new bride and suddenly seemed a dozen years younger as he lifted her veil and kissed her gently upon the lips.

Georgiana wept for joy and wanted to skip and jump about, but she managed to restrain herself for long enough to cast a quick glance at the assembled throng of applauding gentlefolk.

She caught sight of a familiar, finely dressed gentleman at the back of the room, smiling and applauding along with the other nobles. She looked again and recognised Oliver, unaware that he had been personally invited by the Duke to attend the ceremony.

She had, in her time with him, been so focused on discussing his plans for the future, that they had barely mentioned Cordelia's wedding. And, in her conversations with the Duke and her sister, there had been so many important things to attend to, so many changes in her circumstances, that Oliver had not been much mentioned, beyond the Duke's comments on his pleasure at the change in the young man's circumstances.

Yet here he was, looking so elegant, dressed in a splendour suited to his station in life as Marquess of Dartworth, and a welcome guest at the wedding. She could not help but notice that her heart was suddenly beating faster and that she was entirely gladdened by his presence. She smiled and his eyes were instantly upon her.

She could feel the warmth of his smile all the way across the room and his eyes carried something that was much stronger than a simple acknowledgement of her presence. Her mind instantly went back to those stolen moments in the folly, and heat flushed through her.

He held her gaze and she laughed, turning back to the happy couple but glancing back at Oliver to confirm that his attention was entirely focused upon her. If Cordelia was radiant as a new bride, Georgiana felt a wildness in her heart that spoke of freedom and much, much more. She wondered for a moment if the stays in her dress were simply too tight but then she realised that it was Oliver's smile that was leaving her short of breath.

After the wedding, all of the guests made their way to the great ballroom at Canterwood Park, where a veritable feast had been laid out for them to enjoy. The Duke had chosen to make this, at least in part a rather formal occasion and each guest had been allocated a seat according to rank and position.

Georgiana enjoyed watching the expressions of the gossipy members of the *ton,* who had previously so disparaged Oliver, when he took his rightful place at the table, far above many of them. For, as a Marquess, he was, rightfully, second in rank only to the Dukes who were present.

Taking his seat by Georgiana's side, Oliver smiled, happier than he had ever been in society company before. The Duke observed Georgiana and Oliver, then turned to Cordelia with a smile.

"They look comfortable together, don't you think? I would hope that Dartworth will enjoy this feast to the full and keep your sister out of mischief and far away from the menace of chess boards."

Cordelia laughed, simply glad to see Georgiana looking happy, for the first time in weeks.

Georgiana turned slowly to look Oliver over, from head to toe, a light of mischief in her eyes.

"Even more so than the last few days, your attire is exquisite. You seem to have truly forgone your field hand's attire for something more fitting to a Marquess's station in life, my Lord."

"Would you have preferred me in my coarse cloth with mud on my boots and hay between my ears, my Lady?"

"If fine clothing made the man, my Lord, then surely our humble tailors would rule the world."

"My tailor despaired of me and disowned me many years ago, and, indeed, I ceased to be able to afford him anyway. This is the work of the Duke and his generosity."

"So, you cannot claim credit for a good eye for fashion?"

"As you might have noticed from my former attire, I am, without doubt, the world's greatest dunce in matters of fashion, my Lady."

Georgiana laughed, feeling warm, relaxed and safe in his company.

"In truth, I care not what you may wear. It is a man's heart that makes him who he is and no amount of silk collars and silver buttons can improve the contents of a man's heart."

Oliver was silent as he tasted a glass of truly wondrous wine from the Duke's fabled collection.

"And pray tell me, my Lord, what is in your heart at this moment?"

"This is, perhaps, not a suitable place to answer such a question, my Lady."

"Yet I would know the answer, nonetheless."

She was suddenly serious, the game of witty banter abandoned in her plea for openness.

Oliver placed his glass back on the fine damask tablecloth and looked at Georgiana, considering carefully what he might say.

"My Lady, since I have returned to England's shores, my time has been fraught with difficulties. My father's debts left me almost penniless and I had almost given up all hope of seeing my estate restored. In many ways, I faced nothing here but ruin. I thought often enough of returning to the Americas where a man's title has little meaning, to begin again and make my fortune from the rich soil. But, as you know, fortune has favoured me with an unexpected twist and I shall soon be able to pay off my father's debts and restore my house and lands to their former dignity." He paused to taste another sip of the heady vintage. "Perhaps I could rent out my estate now and still pursue my fortune in the Virginias. I could buy land there and grow tobacco. The truth of what is in my heart is that, although I most strongly wish to restore my lands and tenants to a better condition, there is a part of me that is most tempted to simply avoid dealing with the ton completely, and travel again across the ocean to the New World. Perhaps I am deluded, but life there seemed so much simpler than here. And now that we are no longer at war…"

Georgiana gasped and put a hand to her lips. She had not expected such a reply. She had thought, nay she had desperately hoped, that she would hear a much prettier answer to her enquiry.

"You would leave, my Lord?"

"Yes, my Lady. That is what I have been thinking ever since I returned. It is only in this past week that I have seen anything other than unhappiness here."

"But is there nothing, nothing at all, in this great land that might possibly persuade you to stay?"

He looked into her eyes and she thought her heart might stop. She was suddenly oblivious to everyone else in the room. She saw only Oliver. She could hear only his voice. All around them, people were leaving the tables, moving to the part of the room cleared for dancing, or going out onto the terrace for some air. Neither of them noticed any of it.

"I have thought long and hard since we last spoke. The fates have been cruel since I returned to England, and my wishes have turned to bitterness and dust. People have spoken ill of me since my return and, unfairly or not, I do not enjoy a fair reputation. I would not suffer that reputation to be a source of distress to anyone I truly cared for. In the flush of my joy at hearing of your feelings for me, for a moment I truly forgot all of that. But I could not bring such unpleasantness upon you."

"But what if I didn't care at all what people may say or think? What if I truly did not care?"

Oliver smiled again and there was a terrible sadness in his eyes.

"But I care, Georgiana. And I would not be a further cause for gossip. You have endured too much already and I would prefer to believe that a better man than I would make a better husband for you."

He stood to take his leave but Georgiana took his hand quite firmly to stay him, suddenly aware of people moving past them. She was simply not willing to let him cast aside both of their feelings so easily. She had spoken the truth, she cared not one whit for the opinions of others.

"Not so quickly, my slippery Marquess. I am not yet finished with you."

Oliver smiled but there was genuine confusion in his blue eyes. She stood up beside him.

"You owe me a dance, my Lord, for, if I remember correctly, you once offered, over a game of chess, to teach me a few steps, to improve my somewhat poor skills. Since the musicians are preparing to play, I am sure that you will be true to your offer, grant me the honour of a dance."

"My dear Georgiana, by your own admission, you not only cannot dance, but you do not even like to dance."

"Then you will teach me, Oliver. It is high time that I learned."

Chapter Twelve

The evening of the wedding was a spectacular success. The musicians were praised for their playing and the ballroom was full of laughter, gaiety and the stirring rhythms of the most popular dances. The Duke was pleased to demonstrate his nimbleness of foot as he twirled his laughing bride through the line of dancers and the gentlemen cheered him on with raised glasses and a hundred toasts to his health. Georgiana and Oliver had retired to a quieter corner after their careful steps through one of the slower and more stately dances. Oliver was the epitome of patience and never once stepped on his partner's toes for the two hours that they practised together. Gradually, she began to make progress, crediting Oliver with the title of greatest dancing teacher in Christendom for achieving such results.

"Why, Oliver, against all my expectations, I might just learn to enjoy this most difficult of pastimes."

"My Lady, you are possessed of a surfeit of talent that simply required an adequate means of expression."

They both laughed and, held so lightly yet firmly in Oliver's powerful arms, Georgiana felt happier at that moment than she had done in weeks. They had progressed from the simpler country dances to the waltz – a dance which Georgiana had always wished to do well, but had always struggled with, on the few occasions that she had tried. Especially the last, when she had danced that one ill-fated time, with the Earl of Bentwick.

As the ballroom filled and the more experienced dancers displayed their talents, Oliver and Georgiana took up a comfortable seat on a silk-covered couch, and soon found themselves quite lost in their conversation. Georgiana was relieved to find that she seemed to have distracted Oliver from his worries, for now at least. He showed no inclination to leave her side.

When an elderly Viscount approached and asked her to dance, Georgiana smiled most prettily and claimed that she had sprained her ankle and was sadly forced to withdraw from the field of combat, bloodied but unbowed.

Oliver stifled a laugh.

"Would you have been so keen to feign an injury if your suitor had been forty years younger?"

"I am quite done with dancing for the evening, oh my good dancing teacher, and I would prefer to suffer the pleasure of your conversation than the bony hands of the Viscount upon my flesh."

In truth, she found the Oliver's conversation perfectly fascinating. She asked him about his time in the former colonies, about his politics and about his beliefs in the American concepts of liberty and personal freedom.

He displayed an uncommon grasp of the problems of the common people and eloquently expressed his views that the nobility rarely understood the extent to which their prosperity depended on the labour of their tenant farmers. Many seemed to have forgotten that a titled man had as much responsibility, or more, to his tenant farmers, as they had to him.

He was utterly frustrated that they saw his views as revolutionary and damaging – they could not, apparently, conceive of change that did not destroy their way of life. He asked questions of his own and listened most attentively to her answers. He never interrupted or tried to question her views. It was like a breath of fresh air to a young woman who had too often been compelled to conceal her wits and maintain a still tongue in the company of fools.

They teased each other about their drawn chess game, promising to wreak revenge upon each other at the earliest possible opportunity. Georgiana demanded a prize for the winner and to her delight, Oliver readily agreed. There was a warmth between them that she had never felt before, she was transported back, again, to those moments in the stone folly in the gardens, when nothing had seemed more important than being with each other.

As she studied her dashingly handsome companion, she had the sense that Oliver truly accepted her as an equal. It was almost intoxicating and she suspected that she might have to pinch herself occasionally to see if she was dreaming.

As the evening drew to an end and the Duke bowed gracefully to his friends and acquaintances before leading Cordelia from the room, and up the stairs to the privacy of their chambers.

Cordelia looked about for Georgiana, and smiled when she saw her, looking tired but happy, standing with the Marquess of Dartworth. Perhaps Georgiana had found a man to care for, after all.

There was plenty of wine, fresh punch and bottles of excellent cognac to keep the guests refreshed and the musicians were willing to play on until dawn if required. Georgiana tried to stifle a yawn as she rose from her seat.

"Rest assured that it is the hour and not your company that fatigues me, Oliver."

"But you need your rest, my Lady, and I should return to my lodgings in the village or the landlord will suspect I've run away without settling the rest of my account."

They laughed together as he, all propriety in a moment where he dearest wish was to sweep her into his arms, escorted her to where Miss Millpost dozed in a quiet corner – close enough to be regarded as a chaperone, but intruding on no-one.

"Goodnight, fair Georgiana. I cannot thank you enough for the kindness of your heart and the gentleness of your spirit. I am feeling far less unhappy with my lot than I was when we began our conversation this evening."

"Will I see you again soon, Oliver, or must I cause another duel to rouse you from the Inn?"

"Perhaps only time will tell, my Lady."

He reached for her hand, and quite improperly, to her delight, turned it over, and placed a kiss upon her palm, his lips lingering far longer than they should. Warmth spread through her whole body.

"I thought that you wished to be unexceptional, to avoid scandal and gossip, my Lord?"

Her eyes sparkled as she spoke.

"Oh, I do, my Lady, yet in your presence I cannot help but forget myself." He smiled, and his eyes met hers. "I promise you, Lady Georgiana, that I will return for further conversation, and that chess game, and, perhaps, even to be a little improper again, in the very near future."

He raised her hand, which he had not released as they spoke, to his lips and then laid it upon his cheek for a moment. Then he smiled at Georgiana and turned on his heel towards the magnificent marble entrance from where he would summon a groom to bring his horse from the stables.

She watched him leave and, in her heart of hearts, she wondered if she would see him again, if he would be true to his words, or if his disillusionment with the English aristocracy would, in the end, take him from her.

~~~~~

After the week of fairly regular conversations with Dartworth, both Setford and Gerald had reached the conclusion that he was the perfect man for the job that Setford had in mind. With the Duke's wedding done, all of the guests would be leaving, so time was of the essence. They had decided to call upon Dartworth that morning, and raise the subject of him providing such a service to the crown.

The Inn was quiet when they entered, but Dartworth was seated at a table in the small private parlour.
~~~~~

"Good morning, Dartworth. I hope you don't mind us joining you. I have something I'd like to discuss with you."

"Setford, Tillingford – pray, be seated. Although I can't imagine what you would need to discuss with me, I am happy to have your company." They settled at the table and called for coffee. Once they had been served, Setford rose, and closed the door firmly. Dartworth looked at him enquiringly, but said nothing. When Setford had resumed his seat, he spoke quietly.

"Dartworth, I have seen, over the last few weeks, that you are an honourable man, not the revolutionary hothead those foolish gossips would paint you as. I have also seen that you are a man who cares both for his people here, and for the fate of all people. You have seen past the nobility's horror of the common man and frankly assessed the results, good and bad, of what you have seen in the Americas. I value your ability to do that."

"Thank you for your faith in my good sense, my Lord. It is a faith few hold." Setford laughed at Dartworth's dry tone, appreciating the man's ability to assess even himself fairly.

"I am about to ask something of you, which will require every ounce of good sense you have. Let me say, before I ask it, that you are, of course, to do what you wish – this is a request, and it may not sit well with you. But I am hoping that it will, and that you will see your way clear to assist me."

Dartworth obviously found this a startling statement. For so long, others had presumed to try to dictate his path, so that the contrast between them, and the attitude of Baron Setford, now, was shocking.

He nodded, and waited for Setford to continue.

"Dartworth, what I am about to tell you is most confidential. But I trust that you will honour my confidence in you. Let me be blunt. I have, for many years, assisted His Majesty's Government in the gathering and assessment of information. Information that allows our most senior men to make the right decisions, to succeed in sensitive negotiations, and to choose actions that protect our nation. Obviously, that is not a task that I can do alone. Many men assist in this work, each in the way that they are best suited to. Tillingford here, is one of those who works with me, and has given sterling service to his country for many years. He also feels that you are the right person for what I am about to ask of you."

Dartworth shot Gerald a surprised look, wondering just exactly what tasks the man had carried out for the crown.

For, if he understood Setford's words aright, Setford was a spymaster, at the heart of the most secretive part of the country's defence.

"I am, again, honoured by your good opinion of me. I will, of course, honour your trust."

"Excellent. Now, my request is, in itself, fairly simple. I am asking you to travel to America, for some months, to assist me. The peace is still fragile, and the British government would prefer it not be broken. Peace is better for both nations. We believe that there are opportunities to make it stronger. But we need current advice from someone accepted there."

"I will not do anything that leads to more fighting – that would be madness. But am I correct in understanding that you are asking the opposite – you are asking that I provide intelligence that would allow a stronger peace?"

"Exactly m'boy, exactly. There is talk of a new treaty, to remove the threat of naval action on the Great Lakes, and to resolve the continual arguments about the exact border between the United States and British North America. But to negotiate such a thing will be difficult. We would wish to understand the mood of the people there, and know, before we begin, that there is a chance of a successful negotiation. I need a man who understands the place - to go, to observe, and to report back. That's the sum of it. Would you be willing to do this?"

"Why, I would most certainly consider it. I have been thinking that I should, perhaps, go back there, but I am torn – now that I have the means, I want to restore my estates here to good condition. If I went, there would need to be allowance for managing my estates here, somehow, whilst I was gone. And... what reason would I give, for my travel? For to observe, surely, I will need a reason to be there, to talk to many people?"

"Both of those issues can be addressed, I believe. There are men that I know and trust, who could assist with your estates here. And, as for a reason for travel – I have a contact who is a very successful merchant. He is most interested in discovering what trade will and will not work to his business benefit, now, with all this talk of tariffs and constraints. He might even consider travelling with you – your contacts would be as much use to him as to me."

"I will need time to consider this."

"Of course. I expected so. I will call upon you at Dartworth Abbey, a few weeks from now, to hear your decision. Do, please consider this seriously, for, I believe, you can, if you do this, serve the best interests of both the British and the American people."

So saying, Setford rose, they bid each other a polite farewell, and left Dartworth alone, again, musing on this startling conversation over the last of his coffee.

~~~~~

Oliver sat for quite some time, his mind in turmoil. What Setford offered was very tempting – he had judged Oliver's character well – to be able to support something for the benefit of both nations was very appealing. He was so sick of all of the discussions that insisted on the benefit of one at the expense of the other. But... If he went, if he acted upon the idea, rather than just thinking it, he might never see Georgiana again.

He could not bear the idea. In that moment, he realised, quite clearly, that he loved her. That the very idea of spending his life without her was abhorrent. He had been such a fool, being maudlin and bemoaning his situation last night, when he had the chance to spend time with her, when she had, already declared her feelings for him. Now that a chance to actually return to the Americas was presented to him, it no longer seemed so appealing. Yet... he wanted to do as Setford asked, to see people and places again, now with money in his pockets and a chance for a changed life.

He could not, however, make such a choice until he had seen Georgiana – he had to know if she would accept him first.
~~~~~

And, if she would... could she bear for him to be away from her for months? All the tumbled thoughts he had suffered through a night of poor sleep now seemed ridiculous. There was only one thing to do. He must present himself at Canterwood Park without delay.

Chapter Thirteen

The morning after the wedding was cooler, and the sky was heavy with cloud as the day promised rain. Georgiana woke from her deep dreamless sleep with sore feet from her dancing efforts and a feeling of immense sadness, as if she had lost something precious that she might never find again. The chambermaid noted her mood and asked if everything was well with her Ladyship. Georgiana smiled at the girl. Servants, they know and see everything, she thought to herself. There can be no secrets in a great house such as this, with so many eyes constantly watching everything and so many ears listening to every word.

She longed for her own house again. As the chambermaid made up the fire to keep the chill off the room, Georgiana's thoughts drifted back to her lands and she wondered how the people were coping under the new farm manager. Was he a kind man? Or was he another hard-hearted and ruthless slave-driver who only sought profits from the labours of her tenants. She was sure that her estate manager would try to keep things in balance, but still...

The sooner she could return, the better it would be for everyone. Her eyes closed again, and she drifted into a half dreaming state, as the flames crackled in the fire grate and the chambermaid hummed a pretty country tune.

She saw herself in her father's house, the comfortable furniture and familiar items all arranged exactly as she had left them. The windows were freshly cleaned and spotless and bright sunshine was filling the drawing room with beams of warmth and light. Tiny motes of dust floated, golden and sparkling, suspended in the sunlight. Fresh flowers filled the vases on the elegant tables, lending their sweet perfume to the air, blooms that she had cultivated and collected herself, mud on her dress and soil beneath her pretty fingers. She remembered her father's laughter when he saw her, gently chiding her for her peasant girl appearance, smiling at her with all the love a devoted father could muster.

She turned her head in her dream and saw a little girl, a blonde-haired child of about five in a pretty dress, playing with her dolls on the polished floor. Without a word being spoken between them, Georgiana knew instantly that this was her own child, a bright and pretty poppet of a child with wide and curious eyes and a quick and ready smile for her doting mama. The vision filled her heart with so much joy that she felt it would burst. She could not contain her elation. Then she heard a voice in her dream and she turned to see the man who was calling her name. It was Oliver, standing in the doorway with a little boy perched securely on his broad shoulders, their beautiful son and first-born child.

"Mistress?" the voice shattered her dream, bringing her back to the bedchamber at Canterwood Park.

For a moment, she was unsure of where she was and who was calling her.

"Mistress?" The chambermaid was gently calling to wake her. A second maid stood beside her, a girl who normally worked in the downstairs rooms.

"Pardon me, your Ladyship, but you have a visitor waiting downstairs and I was asked to see if you were awake. The visitor is waiting upon you in the drawing room and, may I say that he is a most handsome gentleman indeed."

Georgiana's curiosity was piqued as she tumbled out of her bed and quickly washed herself in the hot water that the chambermaid had just brought to her room. A visitor? She dared not hope, but she dressed as quickly as she could and almost fell to the floor as her dainty shoe caught in the hem of her gown. She calmed herself and took a deep breath before she stepped out of her chambers and walked as gracefully as she could down the long corridor. *'Oh please'*, she thought, *'let it be Oliver!'* She was fighting the urge to run and certainly did not want to trip again and measure her length along the elegantly decorated hallway.

A burly manservant nodded at her approach and silently opened the doors to the elegant drawing room. Miss Millpost was sitting, quiet in the corner, ready to do her duty as chaperone, but Georgiana did not even notice her, for, standing by the fire, with mud flecks on his elegant boots, was Oliver.

Georgiana made a small curtsy, feeling suddenly flustered and unsure. Oliver, looking serious, and somehow very nervous, made his bow to her.

"Good morning, my Lord. Have you risen so early simply to fulfil your promise to me, or do you have other business that you wish to discuss with me?"

Oliver looked at her without speaking, the weight of his words too heavy to escape from his heart. Seeing how serious his face was, Georgiana feared the worst. He was leaving. He had come to the house to bid her farewell. She would never see him again. She stared at him but her vision was partially blurred by the tears that threatened to fall.

"Does my presence so distress you that you are moved to tears, my Lady?"

"I cannot imagine what could possibly cause me to weep." Her voice was tremulous, filled with emotion, and she was having the greatest difficulty maintaining her composure. "Yet if you have ridden all this way to speak to me, pray delay no longer and tell me whatever it is that you wish to say."

Oliver hesitated for a moment before stepping forwards and taking her hands in his. He looked into her tear-filled eyes.

"Dearest Georgiana. I am the world's biggest fool and I have barely slept a wink all night." She looked at him, still uncertain, and a single tear drop landed upon his broad hand. "Georgiana, I cannot imagine a life without you. I love you and cannot think of anything other than being with you." She stared into his beautiful eyes and wondered if it would be possible to drown in those twin pools of blue. "Georgiana," he continued. "My love, my life, will you marry me?"

For a moment, it seemed as if the world had stopped spinning upon its axis. Her breathing had stopped. Her heart had ceased beating.

The birds had stopped singing, and she was certain that they were floating motionless in the damp air. Everything became utterly and completely still. She moved her mouth and it seemed that no words would come out.

And then she forced her lips to move.

"Yes."

The word was ever so softly spoken, barely escaping her mouth, yet it was enough to spin the world instantly back into action. Georgiana took a breath, and said it again, and again, and again, until she was shouting it at the top of her voice. Oliver wrapped her in his arms, spinning her about, holding her so tightly that she thought he might easily snap her stays. And she loved it. They hugged each other like children and then he held her face in his hands and kissed her so gently upon her lips that she thought she would faint completely away and swoon into blissful unconsciousness.

They were laughing with joy as they ran to find Cordelia. Miss Millpost followed, still seeing to propriety, but her face was lit with a smile. Cordelia was endeavouring to create order out of chaos as she organised a small army of servants to pack the bags that would accompany the Duke and his new Duchess on their wedding trip.

"Georgiana! It's a madhouse here and Philip has taken this last opportunity to go hunting with his friends, before they all return to their homes, whilst I attend to the packing."

She was laughing at the absurdity of the situation when she registered Oliver's presence, and his firm grip on her sister's hand. Georgiana appeared to be clinging to that hand as if her life depended upon it.

"Cordelia, I have important news to share. Are you ready? Oliver has proposed." Georgiana rushed the words out, desperate to share her news.

Her sister stared at her as she absorbed the information.

"And I have accepted."

Cordelia continued to stare as if Georgiana was speaking a foreign language.

"We are to be married!"

Suddenly the message made its way beyond the barrier of Cordelia's distracted thoughts of packing and registered fully in her mind.

"You're getting married? To Dartworth?"

"Yes, and you're supposed to congratulate us, you delightfully demented Duchess!"

Cordelia rushed forward to hug her sister and plant a kiss on Oliver's cheek.

"Congratulations to both of you. My stars, Georgiana, you do like to surprise people, do you not? I can't wait to see Philip's face when I give him the news."

The Duke was somewhat less surprised at the news than his new wife, for, after all, only a few days ago, he had given Oliver his blessings when he had hesitantly asked his permission to court Georgiana. He had not expected things to go this far, this fast, but he quickly recovered his composure and offered his hand to Oliver along with a firm slap of congratulations on the Marquess' broad back.

"You have your fortune again, my Lord, and the *ton* are well on their way to accepting you into your rightful place. That brings you both responsibilities and opportunities. The government has a pressing need for men of good character. I believe that many possibilities lie before you. And Lady Georgiana is more than capable of supporting you, in whatever you may do."

He paused as he stroked his chin in contemplation. Oliver wondered, suddenly, if the Duke knew of the offer that Setford had made. Georgiana was beaming and Cordelia shook her head in wonder.

"It seems my husband has taken a liking to you, my Lord, and that fortune has finally shown you the good favour you most surely deserve."

She was looking at her sister and smiling from the depths of her heart, pleased beyond compare to see Georgiana so radiantly happy.

$\sim\sim\sim\sim\sim$

Oliver and Georgiana walked to the stone folly in the gardens, despite the threat of rain, and settled there to talk. Georgiana wondered why he looked serious again, when, moments before, he had been beaming with happiness.

"Georgiana, my love, I have something else to ask you."

She tipped her head to the side, considering him as he spoke, her eyes bright with curiosity, and just a little concern.

"I know that we must talk of our wedding, and when and where that should happen, and a thousand other things, but I have been offered, just this morning, an opportunity which might influence all of that. And I need your opinion on it. For, now, it is not just my decision to make."

Georgiana took his hands in hers and waited, allowing him to explain in his own time. He told her of the offer that Setford had made, that morning, and of his conflicted emotions about it. She could see, in his eyes, and hear, in his tone, how much he wanted to go, to see America again, and to do something worthwhile, that might help so many people if it succeeded. But she could also see how hard it was for him to ask, to place before her the possibility of being away from her, for long months, when they had only just truly found each other. At last, he came to the heart of his question.

"Darling Georgiana, I want to do this. But, if you cannot bear it, I will not go. For you matter more to me than anything. That is what I realised, last night and this morning – all of my other cares and woes are nothing in the face of my love for you. So – it is your choice. Can you bear for me to do this, to go, so soon after we will wed?"

Georgiana smiled, and pulled his head down to her for a kiss, savouring the sweetness of his touch.

"Oliver, though it pains me to even think of being apart from you, I can see how much you want to go. I can live with that. I will have much to do, with Casterfield Grange and Dartworth Abbey to care for – I am certain that I can manage a few months, although I would wish it to be as short a time as possible. And, perhaps you can turn this directly to our advantage too – for perhaps there is an investment opportunity in America?"

A broad smile lit his face, and he hugged her tightly to him, amazed at how lucky he was to have found such a woman.

"I had not thought on that, but, now that I have some funds to work with, you are correct, I would indeed look into such an investment. Your cleverness never ceases to amaze me. Let us, then, arrange things with all speed – if the banns are read this week, we can marry as soon as Cordelia and the Duke return from their travels, for they do not plan to be gone above a month. I want as much time with you before I go as possible!"

A whirlwind of arranging swept them up from that moment, and Baron Setford, in the Duke's absence, proved of remarkable assistance. He was a man who could, it seemed, perform magic, with a quiet word in the right people's ears. His first act was to provide Oliver with a man of business, to assist with his planning for everything – from the wedding, to travel, to the first repairs to Dartworth Abbey. The man was a genius, and, unlike some other men-of-business that Oliver had met, actually respected both his, and Georgiana's, wishes.

<div align="center">~~~~~</div>

A month went by at amazing speed. Cordelia and the Duke returned, refreshed and happy, and Cordelia threw herself into the final stages of the wedding preparations. It was Georgiana's choice to have the wedding in the local church near Casterfield Grange, and the wedding breakfast at Casterfield Grange itself. Cordelia would have preferred to hold the ceremony at Canterwood Downs and the breakfast in the more formal setting of the Duke's grand and elegant house, but she bowed to her sister's wishes.

Faster than she could ever have imagined, the day was upon them.

Their wedding had turned into an alarmingly grand affair, with what seemed half the *ton* attending. It amused Georgiana greatly to see all of these people who had treated Oliver so poorly now celebrating his wedding. It was ridiculous what a difference visible wealth made.

The actual ceremony was simple, and they had both chosen to dress in the most simple and elegant garments possible – no excess ostentation at all. Perhaps they could start a trend for the *ton*, Georgiana thought with amusement, as the vicar finally spoke the words that made them man and wife.

They had chosen to walk the short distance from the church to Casterfield Grange, taking delight in the sun and the fresh air, although it utterly scandalised many of the society women present, who rapidly climbed into their carriages rather than besmirch their hems with dust. Georgiana looked around her, glad to be home – a home that she would share with Oliver, until Dartworth Abbey was fully restored, after which time they would split their time between the two homes.

Despite the unseasonably cold year, Georgiana's roses had bloomed beautifully, and their scent welcomed them as they walked into the house. Her fears about the new farm manager and gardeners had been unfounded, and everything was thriving. She gratefully dropped onto the comfortable couch placed on the terrace, Oliver beside her, and watched as the servants magically produced a fabulous feast of food and drink for their guests. The Duke had opened his celebrated wine cellars and despatched wagonloads of sublime vintages to bless the wedding celebrations.

He had sent his personal pastry chefs and his Spanish coffee master to make sure that the occasion was as lavish and memorable as possible. He did it to please his young wife and her sister, in memory of their father, but also because he felt a sense of obligation to the young Marquess. He had misjudged the man and intended to make good for his error of judgement. There was, he felt, a deep satisfaction in realising that he had, now, actually fulfilled his promises to two dead men. He would rest better knowing those obligations were satisfied, and in such a neat and complementary manner.

After the wedding, Oliver and Georgiana settled into Casterfield Grange, as Dartworth Abbey was still barely habitable, although Oliver did spend some time there, ensuring that the repairs were proceeding apace. Baron Setford had, in his usual unassumingly efficient way, produced a gentleman of excellent background, a close associate of Gerald Otford, the new Baron Tillingford, who was available to reside at Dartworth Abbey, and take on the care of the place for the time that Oliver was away.

Setford had explained his availability as a combination of a wish to be away from his family, and a need to be doing something, now that he had returned from the war in France. As the second son of an Earl, there were few socially acceptable occupations available. Oliver had liked the man at once. Lord Barton Seddon was quiet, but astute, and his obvious courtesy and care for others recommended him. The man also, apparently, had a keen eye for horseflesh, and wanted to breed them. That was an activity that Oliver could wholeheartedly support. An arrangement had quickly been made, to everyone's satisfaction, and now the time of Oliver's departure was approaching at speed.

He was glad that, in his absence, the house that his father had neglected, with its grand ballroom and beautiful reception rooms, would be fully restored. Oliver and Georgiana often talked deep into the night, of their plans for the future and the ways in which they might increase the prosperity of their lands and their tenants. They had decided, after considerable thought, that Oliver would, whilst in America, seek out land to buy in Virginia or possibly further north, to create a plantation that would also add to their wealth.

His departure only a week away, Oliver's excitement was growing. He would miss Georgiana terribly, but he could not deny his enthusiasm for seeing again, the place that had, in so many ways, been the making of him. A message arrived one evening, from Baron Setford, informing Oliver that the merchant he had mentioned, Mr. Raphael Morton, on whose business Oliver would ostensibly be travelling, had decided to travel with him, and that Setford would bring the man to Casterfield Grange to meet him, the following day.

~~~~~

Raphael followed Setford up the steps to the door of the pleasant manor in Berkshire, wondering if he would like this man he had agreed to travel with. Gerry had assured him that the man was good and honourable, honest and forthright, in a way that he was certain Raphael would appreciate. He had taken his word for it. In truth, Raphael's thoughts were mostly elsewhere. This chance to do more travel, to see more of the places that his ship's captains told him of when they returned with rich cargoes, was something he had grabbed at, upon Setford's suggestion.
~~~~~

But he knew, in his heart, that he was going for the wrong reason. There were things here in England he needed to resolve, if he were ever to be truly happy again. He just didn't know how to solve those problems. So, if he was honest with himself, he would have to say that, right now, he was running away from his problems, instead of facing them. Ludicrous at his age, but there you have it. It was the truth.

They were greeted at the door by the Marquess and his wife, who were both happily informal with him, and, unusual indeed for the nobility, seemingly unconcerned that he was untitled, a merchant who sullied his hands with trade on a daily basis. He was used to being treated with disdain, despite the fact that he was far, far wealthier than most of the titled men he had met. Raphael felt the tension begin to drain out of him. Perhaps this journey might be quite pleasant after all.

"May I present Mr. Raphael Morton, owner of the renowned 'Morton Empire Imports'. Raphael, the Marquess and Marchioness of Dartworth."

Raphael bowed, and then was surprised when the Marquess stepped forward to take his hand in greeting.

"Please, Mr. Morton, Raphael, if I may, let us dispense with formality between us. My name is Oliver, please feel free to address me as such. If we are to travel together, it would seem ridiculous not to be on friendly terms."

"I thank you, Oliver, for your kindness."

Oliver laughed, a cheerful and unaffected sound. "I assure you, it is you who are kind to me, travelling with me, providing me passage on your ship, and providing me a reason to be where Baron Setford wishes me to be."

The Marchioness spoke up, in a bright friendly voice.

"Come gentlemen, let us repair to the parlour. It may be summer, but it is still not so warm standing here upon the doorstep! And Mr. Morton, please do call me Georgiana – I am also fond of a rather shocking lack of formality." Her smile lit her face, and, for a moment, although they were, in almost all ways, strikingly different, it reminded him of Sera. His heart ached a little in his breast.

Allowing himself to be herded into an elegant parlour, he pushed such thoughts aside, and concentrated on the man he had come to meet. Two hours later, they were all completely comfortable with each other, and Raphael had learned much of Oliver's history. His respect for the man grew, the more he learned. But it was time to leave – in a few days' time, he would set off with this man for a journey of months – enough time to talk then. He rose, Setford with him, and prepared to take his leave.

"Oliver and Georgiana, I must thank you wholeheartedly for your hospitality. I look forward to our journey. And, Oliver, one other thing I feel I must say. I am grateful to you, for taking up Setford's suggestion, and agreeing to Lord Barton Seddon caretaking your estate in your absence. Bart has not had a good time of it, since we returned from war. You have given him a greater gift than you can imagine."

~~~~~

Setford smiled to himself, saying nothing as the carriage returned them to London. Everything was working out very nicely, very nicely indeed.
~~~~~

Epilogue

Four years later – August 1820.

The fields were ripening with wheat and barley and oats as Georgiana, Marchioness of Dartworth, looked out across the sunlit landscape of her beloved estate and smiled. The orchards were full of fruit and she was looking forward to harvesting the ripening crop of plums and cherries to make preserves, that would remind them of summer's sweetness in the long winter months to come. A lingering taste of a glorious summer and a hint of the happiness that she shared with her loving husband.

She ran her hand over her swollen abdomen and thought of the birth of their next child, a blessing to come in the late days of October. Her pretty little daughter was playing with her dolls on the perfectly polished floor of the drawing room. Her blonde hair caught the sunlight and her laughter could be heard throughout the great household.

"Charlotte, my darling, it is time for you to put your dollies back in the doll's house and tell Cook that we are ready for luncheon. Will you run and tell her for me, please?"

Charlotte scrambled to her feet, scooping her dolls up into her small arms and depositing them in a tangled heap inside the beautifully carved doll's house. At just two years old she was still a little unsteady on her feet at times, but never fussed unduly. If she tumbled over, she simply picked herself up and continued. She ran to the kitchens to be scooped up in her turn by the household's cook, who lifted her high and held her aloft like a bird in flight. She was so much like her mother, and had certainly inherited her intelligence and sense of independence. And everyone simply adored her.

"Tell your mama that luncheon will be served in five minutes, my poppet. Now run, run, run and tell her!"

The kitchen staff laughed at the little girl's serious look as she sped off on her short little legs, a bundle of energy and joy that captivated everyone's hearts.

Charlotte was panting as she held her mother's knees.

"Mama? What you said this morning, is it true? Is Papa really coming home today?"

Georgiana smiled.

"Why, yes, I most certainly hope so, my angel, and we shall be most pleased to see him, won't we?"

Charlotte clapped her hands in excitement just as her son's elderly tutor knocked on the drawing room door and respectfully announced, with a small bow, that the morning's lessons had been concluded.

Georgiana opened wide her arms as her son and first-born child bounded into the room to give her a mighty hug. At nearly four, he was happy, bright and intelligent.

"And what has young William learned today, Master Hobbs?"

"His mastery of the game of chess is progressing well, your Ladyship, and his language skills grow apace. But he shows too little application to the science of mathematics and may, regrettably, be lost to the art of Euclid."

Whilst most might find this a remarkable range of topics for a boy so young to study, Georgiana had seen no reason not to feed his amazing capacity to learn. The true complexities of the subjects he would learn in later years, but his grasp of the basics was already astonishing for his age. In response to Master Hobbs comment, Georgiana laughed.

"William, how do you expect to run the estate if you cannot calculate your sums and understand geometry?"

"But Mama, classical history and philosophy is so much more interesting. And if I need help with my sums, I can always engage the services of my tutor."

"You see, your Ladyship? William has the wit to pardon every oversight and shortcoming. He will undoubtedly go far in this world."

"Pray, good Master Hobbs, would you care to join us for lunch? I should like to hear you converse with William and demonstrate for me his newly acquired skills in languages other than English."

"With the greatest of pleasure, your Ladyship. The boy truly has a rare gift for languages both ancient and modern."

Georgiana nodded her agreement with his assessment.

Suddenly there was a commotion in the grand entrance hall and Georgiana turned her head to see what could be the source of the fuss and noise.

A footman opened the drawing room doors and in strode Oliver, the dust on his attire indicating that he had, at just that moment, arrived from London. He was smiling with joy as he gathered his son and daughter into his arms and hugged them.

"Papa, your whiskers are tickling my face!" shrieked Charlotte, but Oliver refused to let go of her, and his precious little daughter was obviously delighted to be swept up in her loving father's arms. William had been a precocious child from the start, being the result of the intense month which they'd had, between their marriage, and Oliver's journey to America, with Raphael. Oliver had been overjoyed to return, and discover that, soon, he would be a father.

Now, William had his head pressed against his father's chest as Oliver stroked his hair. The group might have stayed in that position for hours, except that, at that moment, Cook knocked loudly upon the open door to announce that luncheon was served. Oliver stood and went to his beautiful wife, kneeling at her side and folding his arms around her. He was too overcome to speak.

"I do declare that I have missed you terribly, my love."

She spoke the words quietly in her husband's ear and he breathed in the perfume of her hair and skin and rejoiced in his heart that he was home at last.

"Come." He said at last. "Let us all eat, for I am starving and in need of sustenance, and the light of your sweet company."

They rose together to discover what Cook had prepared to surprise their palates for lunch. Whatever it was, it would surely taste all the better for the presence of the head of the household. Oliver was home, and Georgiana's heart was filled with joy.

The Prince Regent was finally crowned King, a full six months after his father's death, and the business of the nation had settled into a calmer state. Oliver had spent much of the last four years, since his return from America in January of 1817, as a respected advisor to Setford and others.

His estates were more profitable than they had ever been in his father's time, his plantation in America had proven a remarkably good investment, and his ongoing business dealings with Raphael had been of great benefit to both of them. Add that to the ever-increasing prosperity of the lands of Casterfield Grange and he was a very wealthy man.

He had, at the end of this long session of politicking, finally declared to Setford that he wished to remove himself from London, and, for quite some time to come, devote himself fully to the needs of his growing family. Whilst this was a rather outrageous thing for a member of the nobility to do, Oliver, as usual, gave not one whit of care for their opinions.

"You won't be going to London anymore, my dear?"

Georgiana was as surprised at her husband's announcement as the children were excited.

"Only to enquire about the latest ladies' fashions from Paris, for your benefit," he replied with a grin.

"I am home at last and this is where I intend to stay, whether we are at Dartworth Abbey or here at Casterfield Grange, so long as I am with you, I will be happy."

William could hardly contain his excitement. "Papa, you promised to take me fishing. When may we go?"

"We must first consult with Master Hobbs here and determine whether you have applied yourself diligently to your studies. Then, perhaps, we might find a day to explore the river and see if we can tease a pair of fine trout from the water."

William clapped his hands in excitement and Oliver could clearly imagine the blessing of spending a day with his son on a quiet riverbank, teaching him the art of fishing.

After lunch, as the children took a short nap and Master Hobbs applied himself to his writing, armed with a glass of sherry, a pipeful of good tobacco and a freshly sharpened quill, Oliver sat with his wife and talked of the future.

"My darling, when the baby has been born and you have your strength back, mayhap next year, I am mindful to make a journey and I want you and the children to come with me."

Georgiana's curiosity was piqued by the suggestion.

"A journey, Oliver? And what would be the purpose and destination to such a journey?"

"I'm of a mind to visit our estates in America, my love, and show you how great the Americas have become in so short a time. To show you how different a place it is from here. To show you the places where I learned to labour for my own survival, and appreciate the work of others."

"Oliver, you speak of a long journey and many months away from our home."

There was a hint of consternation in Georgiana's voice.

"Indeed, that is true, but I would not make the journey without you. I could not bear to be away from you for that long, again. Once was quite enough." They were quiet as the idea sank in and the implications of such a long voyage sparked further questions. Oliver continued, "I am free of my duties and responsibilities to the government and am ready to take advantage of my new freedom. Only think on it, my darling, for we could not consider leaving for at least another year."

"And what of William's education? Would he have to learn to become a sailor on the long voyage to the Americas? I had hoped for more for his future." Oliver laughed, as Georgiana could always make him do.

"Oh, no, my love. William will not be serving his passage as a cabin boy or a powder monkey! I fully intend bringing Master Hobbs along with us too, so that William's education will not be neglected in any way. But I feel he would learn much from a visit to the New World, lessons that cannot be found in his books."

Georgiana smiled. An adventure. A trip to the New World. A chance to explore an entirely different society. Despite her profound attachment to her lands and her beautiful house, the spirit of adventure still touched her heart. She said that she would think on it, but deep within her heart she had already made up her mind. If they were away for even a full year, she knew that both Casterfield Grange and Dartworth Abbey would be well cared for, by people they trusted and loved.

As long as she was with Oliver and the children she would go anywhere in the world, and know that she would always be happy.

Her life had changed so much since that cold, Spring day, when she had accompanied her sister to the Duke's magnificent house, to see Cordelia married, and to find a husband for herself.

No-one could have foreseen how her life would be.

No-one could have predicted that the penniless and mud-soiled Marquess of Dartworth would confound everyone's expectations, reclaim his fortune and win the hand of Lady Georgiana Branley in marriage.

No one could have foreseen how exquisitely happy she would become in the arms of her husband and family.

Now perhaps she was ready for another adventure, to sail into the unknown and see first-hand the place that had so strongly formed her husband's opinions on life. Yes, it would be an adventure. But she would be safe in the arms of her husband, Oliver Kentworthy, Marquess of Dartworth - and that was worth more than all of their estates put together.

The End

Arietta Richmond
Regency Historical Romance

About the Author

Arietta Richmond has been a compulsive reader and writer all her life. Whilst her reading has covered an enormous range of topics, history has always fascinated her, and historical novels been amongst her favourite reading.

She has written a wide range of work, from business articles and other non-fiction works (published under a pen name) but fiction has always been a major part of her life. Now, her Regency Historical Romance books are finally being released. The Derbyshire Set is comprised of 10 novels (7 released so far). The 'His Majesty's Hounds' series is comprised of 12 novels, with the sixth having just been released.

She also has a standalone longer novel shortly to be released, and two other series of novels in development.

She lives in Australia, and when not reading or writing, likes to travel, and to see in person the places where history happened.

Be the first to know about it when Arietta's next book is released!

Sign up to Arietta's newsletter at

http://www.ariettarichmond.com

When you do, you will receive a free copy of the <u>subscriber exclusive</u> novella **'A Gift of Love',** a prequel to the Derbyshire Set series, which ends on the day that 'The Earl's Unexpected Bride' begins

This story is not for sale anywhere – it is absolutely exclusive to newsletter subscribers!

Here is your preview of

Finding the Duke's Heir

His Majesty's Hounds – Book 7
Sweet and Clean Regency Romance

Arietta Richmond

Chapter One

Julian Stafford, Duke of Windemere, signed the document with a flourish. Hopefully, that was the last. His wife, Antonia, had been dead for over a year now, yet here he was still paying the debts that she had incurred. He pitied the modistes, shopkeepers and jewellers she had patronised. When she had been still living, he'd had no idea that they were not being paid. And, it seemed, they had been so afraid of asking for their due, that it had taken some of them a year to come forward.

When the ink had dried on the page, Julian handed the document to his man of business, who had stood patiently waiting whilst he dealt with it.

"I hope that is the last, Burrowes. But, if more of them come forward, bring their claims to me, as always. For now, see these paid. Why it has taken them so long to come forward escapes me. Surely I am not so terrifying a figure that they would expect to have their due claims denied?"

Burrowes shook his head sadly.

"Your Grace, I believe that your late wife was rather harsh in her dealings with those of the merchant classes. It seems reasonable that they should judge you by what they saw of her, if unfair. After all, they have never met you."

"True, Burrowes, although a distressing thought. I hate to think of the hardship that some of these people undoubtedly suffered, simply because my wife could not bestir herself to arrange payment of her bills. Please, ensure that any tradesmen and shopkeepers that my estates deal with are always paid promptly in future. I do not wish to emulate so many of the *ton*, and spend without the ability, or intention, to pay."

"As you wish, Your Grace."

Burrowes bowed, and took his leave, stack of papers in hand. Julian sat back in his chair, staring, unseeing, as the early afternoon sun cast beams of light past the curtains and onto the magnificent woven silk rug upon his study floor.

A few motes of dust sparkled like gold dust in the sunbeams, but Julian didn't see them – his thoughts were elsewhere, in his mind he saw, yet again, the day when Martin was brought home on a hurdle, the life already fled from his body, blood everywhere. His son and heir, his only child, gone, and in a way that need never have happened.

How different might his own life have been now, if Antonia had been able to see past her prejudice and disdain for the lower classes, and accept Martin's choice. If she had accepted Marion, then others might never have disparaged her to Martin's face, the duel might never have happened, and Martin might still be here with him.

Julian shook himself out of his thoughts. Foolish maundering - such thinking would only leave him blue-devilled for no useful reason. He could not change the past. Still, he did wonder what had happened to Marion. For he had neither seen, nor heard anything of, either her, or her family, since the day of Martin's death. It disturbed him. He wished that he might have helped her, to honour Martin's choice, no matter how much that would have offended Antonia, but one cannot help a woman one cannot find.

~~~~~

At the same moment that Julian stared unseeing at sunbeams, not so far away, in her private parlour in Pendholm House, Lady Sylvia Edgeworth, Dowager Viscountess Pendholm, also sat staring at sunbeams. Lady Sylvia, however, was very aware of the sun. She was grateful for the late spring sunshine, with the promise of actual warmth this summer, unlike the previous year. She did wonder, however, what she would be doing this summer.

She had chosen to stay in London, when her son, Lord Charlton Edgeworth, Viscount Pendholm, and his wife, Lady Odette, had retired to their country estate, Pendholm Hall, for the summer. It was time she gave Charlton and Odette the space to be themselves, without her presence intruding. Pendholm House felt so empty now, with Charlton and Odette gone, and Harriet, now married to Lord Geoffrey Clarence, also gone.

Lady Sylvia was overjoyed that her children had both found such happiness, but now found herself rather lost.
~~~~~

She could visit Mary and the other girls, and their delightful children, regularly, but they also needed time to themselves.

With most of the *ton* leaving town as summer approached, there were less and less social events, less and less people to call upon and, therefore, less and less things with which to fill her days.

If she was honest, Lady Sylvia did not care at all about the lack of society events. They had become rather boring.

The more time she spent with Mary, Sally, Poppy and Rose, seeing the vast transformation in their lives which had been wrought by something so simple as having given them a decent home to live in, enough food to eat, and a small number of staff to help them care for their children, the more she wished to bring that kind of transformation to others.

The suffering of the lower classes, especially those girls who had been abused by their employers, then cast out, had become more real to her, as she came to understand what those lives were really like. No woman should suffer such treatment.

And, certainly, no child should be raised in the sort of appalling conditions that Mary and Rose had been living in, when Lady Sylvia had found them. Especially no grandchild of hers, regardless of which side of the blanket they were born on!

With bitter sadness, she yet again acknowledged that she was, truly, glad that her eldest son was dead. The only positive things he had left in her life were the children, and an adequate supply of money to assist them.

Deciding to help other girls like Mary was one thing. Knowing where to start, to do so, was another entirely.

But… she most definitely needed something to do with her time, and far better something useful, than a genteel and useless occupation. Never prone to being still for long, Lady Sylvia rose, and went to her escritoire. Swiftly, she penned a note to Lady Anna Trubridge, Viscountess Farnsworth, Odette's aunt, and, of late, Lady Sylvia's closest friend.

~~~~~

Two hours later found Lady Sylvia comfortably ensconced in Lady Farnsworth's parlour, with a cup of excellent tea, and some delightful small cakes. Just being in Anna's cheerful company made Lady Sylvia feel far better. Anna had an acerbic wit, and a clear, if somewhat unforgiving, view of the world around her. She was not afraid to express her opinions, and her astute observations not only entertained, but frequently informed in a way that Lady Sylvia found invaluable.

"So, my dear, what can I do for you today? Whilst your company is delightful at any time, I sense that something is troubling you. Do tell – for today has been rather boring so far."

"Dear Anna, I have an idea. And I want your opinion." Lady Farnsworth looked enquiringly at Lady Sylvia, waiting for her to continue. "I have been thinking a lot of late. Frankly, I need something to do. Now that both Charlton and Harriet are happily leading their own lives, they don't really need me."

"I can see how that would leave your days rather empty, for indeed, my days have become the same. Now that Odette is happily married to Charlton, and learning to run her own establishment, as a Viscountess should, I am alone for the first time in many years. It is a strange feeling, is it not?"
~~~~~

"Yes. Most definitely. I do not want to become one of those horrible society widows, whose life descends into a dull round of soirees where nothing is spoken but gossip and petty recrimination." Lady Sylvia shuddered at the thought, her green brown eyes sparkling with the intensity of her emotion.

"I cannot ever imagine you being like that, even if you tried to be! You are far too kind a soul. You lack the sharpness of tongue required to play such a part, dear Sylvia."

"I am glad that you think so! The challenge I have faced, dear Anna, is one of finding something to do – anything to do – which might be regarded as a suitable activity for a Lady of my position, and which is not unmitigatedly dull and boring. I have, finally, had an idea. I want to help more girls like Mary, Rose, Sally and Poppy. You have seen how much better their lives are, for what we have given them – which seems so little to us. Surely there are many other girls in situations like theirs, who need help? I think that I will spend the rest of my life wanting to help those abused by their noble employers – it might, in some small part, make up for the terrible things that my son did, whilst he lived. The problem is, I don't know how to start."

"That is a very good idea! Perhaps Mary and the girls can advise us on how we might find others who need help?"

"Of course! Shall we visit them now?"

Chapter Two

The ale was cool, and the food was good. Charles Barrington, Viscount Wareham, had stayed in the Marston Arms Inn many times over the past few years, and the innkeeper made sure that he was well served. Charles was happy. Soon, he could return to Meltonbrook Chase, and be close to Lady Maria again. His business on Hunter's estates was concluded for this visit, with everything in order, and excellent potential for a good harvest this year – a pleasant change from the previous year.

Only one thing marred his satisfaction with the world. It was nigh on four years now, and he had still not fulfilled his promise to Scartwick. A promise made as the man lay dying, after a senseless duel. That duel was one of the things that had convinced Charles that the London life was not for him. He cared more for his brother's estates than for drinking and gambling. But Scartwick had charged him with protecting Marion – and he had failed – not only had he not protected her, he hadn't even found her... yet.

He would not give up. He still, every day, brought out the folded paper that Scartwick had thrust into his hand as he died. The paper that proved, unarguably, that Marion was Scartwick's wife. He looked at it again then, frustrated, put it away. As he did, a snippet of overheard conversation came back to him, from earlier that day.

He had been finishing up his meeting with the farm manager at Hunter's Springmarsh estate, when three of the farm labourers had returned from the fields. Their talk was of the sad death of an old woman who had lived in a nearby village. She had, apparently, been Nanny to two or three generations of the local aristocracy, and been well liked by everyone. The last part of their conversation, however, was what struck him most. One of them had said *'What d'ye think'll happen to the daughter and granddaughter now, with the old woman gone? I never understood why that granddaughter hasn't got herself a husband to look after them. She's three and twenty, and good to look at, but she's by herself, with a three-year-old child that is, apparently, hers. Well, that's what happens to people in London – better she'd never lived there, if you ask me.'*

The words stuck in his mind. It seemed a very long stretch of possibility. Yet... Marion would be three and twenty by now. And with a child... if he let himself believe the outlandish possibility that it could be Marion they spoke of, then a child of three would be the right age – the right age to be Scartwick's child... Could that be why he'd found no trace of Marion in nigh on four years – because he was looking for a woman alone, not a woman with a small child, living with her mother?

The idea gnawed at him. He had to know for sure.

Another day here would not change anything at home. But… if it was Marion, it could change his life, and her's. He could fulfil his promise to Scartwick, and be free of it.

The Innkeeper was glad of the money that providing another night's lodging brought him, and the following morning Charles hurried back to Springmarsh, and enquired after the labourers. The farm manager apologised, explaining that the men were not there – he had sent them with the farm cart to the next town, to deliver promised supplies to a merchant of the town.

Inwardly cursing, Charles thanked the man, and set off, towards Meltonbrook Chase after all – he could not, reasonably, stay another two or three days to await their return. But he would be back. Any possibility of finding Marion, however slim, he would follow to its end.

<div align="center">~~~~~</div>

Jane Canfield had never felt older. Grief and exhaustion had left her feeling empty, almost hopeless. The only thing that motivated her to continue was her daughter, and her grandson. The grandson who, oblivious to everything else, played happily with a pile of wooden blocks, which he had scattered across the worn rug at her feet.

It did not matter that she did not know who they boy's father was, that Marion still refused to tell her, had always answered *'It doesn't matter now'*, when she had asked. She loved the child anyway, as she loved her daughter - the daughter who had arrived on her doorstep, expecting and alone, nearly four years ago.

Continuing to watch Daniel, Jane spoke softly.

"How will we go on now, Marion? Now that your grandmother is gone. I know that she is better off with God, for this last year has been hard, where she didn't even remember us, really, and kept calling Daniel by the name of the boy she cared for when I was a child." Jane sighed, still watching the child, before she continued. "The only reason we have survived the last two years is the charity that the Countess was kind enough to send my mother, as thanks for all of her years of service to the family. And mother's cottage is theirs – now she's gone, it will be given to some other dependent of the Earl of Morcross. All we have is this little cottage of our own, a few things that my mother owned, and us. I don't know, now, how we'll feed ourselves, let alone a growing boy."

Marion turned and hugged her mother to her, the glitter of unshed tears in her eyes.

"We'll find a way, Mother, somehow, we will."

Get

"Finding the Duke's Heir"

as soon as it's released – go to
http://www.ariettarichmond.com

and make sure that you are signed up for news and release notices!

Books in the 'His Majesty's Hounds' Series

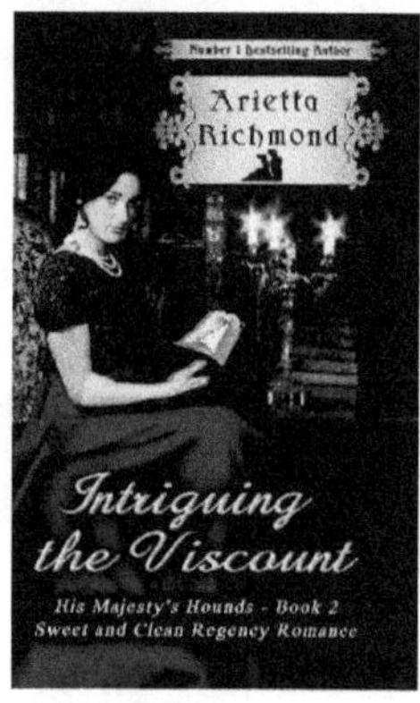

Winning the Merchant Earl (coming soon)

Healing Lord Barton (coming soon)

Loving the Bitter Baron (coming soon)

Rescuing the Countess (coming soon)

Attracting the Spymaster (coming soon)

Books in 'The Derbyshire Set'

The Marchioness' Second Chance (Coming Soon!)

Lady Theodora's Christmas Wish

The Derbyshire Set Omnibus Edition Vol. 1 (the first three books all in one)

The Derbyshire Set Omnibus Edition Vol. 2 (the second three books all in one)

Available at all good book stores and for ebook readers too!

Regency Collections with Other Authors

Coming in August 2017!

Other Books from Dreamstone Publishing

Dreamstone publishes books in a wide variety of categories – here are some of our other bestselling books:-

We have books in many categories, ranging from Erotica and Romance to Kids Books, Books on Writing, Business Books, Photography, Cook Books, Diaries, Coloring books and much more. New books are released each month.

Be the first to know when our next books are coming out

Be first to get all the news – sign up for our newsletter at

http://www.dreamstonepublishing.com